BLEEDTHROUGH

AND OTHER SMALL HORRORS

SCARLETT R. ALGEE

ISBN: 978-1-7343897-0-8 (sc)
ISBN: 978-1-7343897-1-5 (ebook)
Library of Congress Control Number: 2020902227

First printing edition: May 26, 2020
Published by Cold War Radio Press in the United States of America.
Cover Design and Layout: Don Noble/Rooster Republic Press

Cold War Radio Press
201 Lake Street
Ridgely, TN 38080

AUTHOR'S NOTE:
SOME OF THESE STORIES DEAL WITH SENSITIVE TOPICS.
CONTENT WARNINGS ARE PROVIDED IN PUBLICATION HISTORY.

BLEEDTHROUGH

AND OTHER SMALL HORRORS

HALF-PAST

THREE MINUTES AFTER midnight Nassa thrashes in the bed and wakes herself coughing, painfully pushing her thin frame upright to fumble at the rusty sludge oozing from the corner of her mouth, and Phenia knows it's time.

On her way to the kitchen, she plucks the tiny ornate clock from the mantel. It had been Nassa's gift to her for their wedding fifty years ago: crafted across the sea, the dark strange-grained wood ornamented with scrollwork and carved roses. Priceless, precious, unfailingly accurate even now.

Phenia puts the kettle on to boil and holds the little clock between her hands, watching the second hand tick round, whispering over the gurgle of roiling water the words of the enchantment she'd laid on it at sunrise, hoping it will be enough.

When the kettle shrills, she tucks the clock into a pocket of her skirt and reaches far back into the cupboard, drawing out the jar of black powder she's so carefully hidden from Nassa, even though her wife hasn't left her bed in days. Hasn't done anything but cough and sleep and twist fitfully as the cancer eats away at her.

They have not discussed this plan, because Phenia has been terrified that Nassa would say no.

Phenia empties the jar into a large cup and adds the boiling water, stirring carefully and wincing as the odor of sweet rot reaches her nostrils. The ingredients had been surprisingly easy to obtain: gravedust; henbane; powdered bone. Two petals from the bouquet of never-die roses she'd given Nassa on their first anniversary, still as vibrantly pink and glossy as they'd been five decades earlier. Only the corpse-tongue had proven difficult—not the small black flower that clusters around new graves, but the literal object, and that less than three days old—but last night a dose of laudanum had made Nassa sleep soundly enough for Phenia to have a midnight prowl and find a drunken vagrant, and that, thanks to a particularly sharp boning knife, had been that.

This sleep will be more profound, though what happens after is less certain. Nassa coughs again, and Phenia lifts the cup and starts up the stairs.

***

There is blood on the coverlet. Nassa has fallen back on her pillows, dull-eyed and panting, but she still scrabbles fruitlessly at the stain.

"It's all right." Phenia sets the steaming cup on the bedside table and sits on the edge of the bed, catching her wife's hand in both of her own and gently squeezing the thin, hard-edged fingers. Nassa had been a scribe when they'd married, and she'd had such beautiful hands. "Do you think you can sit up again? I brewed something for your cough."

"Try." Nassa's voice is all but gone, but with a huge effort and Phenia's arm around her shoulders, she gets upright. "So tired."

"I know, love." Phenia takes the cup and guides it to Nassa's lips. "Drink this and you can sleep again."

After the first mouthful, throat eased by heat and moisture, Nassa draws back in reproach. "Everything you brew is unaccountably vile."

"I know." Phenia dips her head in apology; the little clock is still a weight in her pocket, its ticks palpable against her thigh. "But it works."

"Vain thing." Nassa laughs hoarsely and drinks again, drinks until she's breathless. She lies back, breathing hard. "Enough."

Phenia draws the cup away and inspects the contents. Enough indeed, she agrees silently, and sets it down, running her fingers through the patchy remnants of her wife's iron-grey hair until Nassa's breathing deepens and slows. Then a hitch, a final cough, and it ceases altogether.

For a long moment, in what feels like solidarity, Phenia holds her breath. Touches Nassa's mouth and nostrils and throat, assures the presence of neither breath nor pulse. Then she pulls the miniature clock free and sets it on the table.

Half past midnight. The hands have gone still.

But as Phenia watches, wondering if the enchantment took hold, wondering if there's space within the teeth of the nesting gears for her spouse and lover's soul, the ivory numbers inset in the dial begin to glow, one by one: green, like Nassa's eyes. The golden hands jerk forward once, then backward, and the entire device wobbles uneasily; then it stills, and the hands tick forward again, and time goes on.

Phenia lets out her breath. "I'm sorry," she whispers, speaking not to her wife's still, pallid face, but to the clock's dial. "I'm sorry. I know you're probably angry right now, but you would have said no if I'd asked, and I can't be without you. Not yet. Not after so long. So I didn't ask."

She stops, staring at the numbers, which are still luminescent. The *tick-tock* has gone hollow.

"I didn't ask," she repeats, and reaches for the cup. Perhaps it will be enough. Perhaps where there's room for one soul, there will be room for two, ground together in the mechanism, tick by tick.

Phenia drains the cup and watches the clock.

BLACK, RED, BLACK

FAR OFF DOWN the boulder-strewn plain, she sees them coming, arcing black shapes against the greenish light of the mist-shrouded sun.

He gurgles. She looks down; she'd thought him gone already, and picks up her crimson skirts to step back from the darker flood that's escaped his throat. Another upward hitch of the vermilion silk, bunching it around the blade still dripping in her hand, and she plants one bare foot flat on his chest, then the other. Under her left sole something creaks and yields; his noises grate the air and die away.

He should have known better, really. Should have listened, should have had the sense not to go looking in the dark corners of the house that she'd forbidden. Then he wouldn't have found that door in the cellar.

Or the six graves full, with the seventh grave waiting.

She lifts the knife to her ruby lips and licks it clean, feeling gore stiffen and dry down her chin. In the sickly light his face is slack and soft-eyed, his mouth relaxed now into something that's not quite a smile, and she shifts her weight, a Kali balancing atop Shiva.

The first crow screams, approaching. She drops her skirts and lifts her arms, silver blade and crimsoned smile flashing in the face of the waning sun, and calls back a hoarse raw welcome to the feast. The birds stream around her, midnight plumage and jewel-bright eyes, claws and beaks tearing fabric and flesh alike. She only laughs and casts the knife aside, stripping the blood from one scratched forearm with the edge of her hand and shoving her fingers into her mouth.

Above her, above him, the birds wheel, and gather, and then descend.

STRONG AS MARBLE, WARM AS BLOOD

SHE IS PERFECT, because I made her so.

Only my hands have worked the blue-veined, dove-grey marble I chose for her body. Only I look upon the fluting of her cheekbones and the impeccable dimpling beneath her lower lip, the width of every eyelash, every strand of every curl that falls over her forehead and tumbles to her waist. Only I have weighed the curves of her breasts and squeezed the span of her hips so often that their dimensions are like old acquaintances.

Delicately I hollowed out her nostrils, the near-translucent edges of her ears, seeking to put into her every ounce of the divine ideal I never yet discerned in her fleshly, breathing counterparts. I counted off every hair in each eyebrow, rasped her nails and the edges of her philtrum to fingertip-width perfection, measured out the space between her thighs.

And then, then, the final thing: paying out coin to whores who were baffled by my need to sketch their secret parts, accepting their scorn that I might chisel out all her intimate depths and polish their surfaces to glistening—that I might test them and count myself satisfied.

And now—I pray, I sacrifice, that the gods who once breathed life into a handful of dust can breathe it into this woman I coaxed forth from stone, whose sleek limbs gain more sheen with each sanding.

Because she is perfect. Because she is everything.

With another prayer upon my lips I splay my hand across the cool concavity of her belly, trace my thumb over the dip of her navel. Do I imagine the shudder in the marble, the flush of warmth beneath my palm?

But I look at her face and see color breaking out amid the grey, the drape of her hair softening as black spreads out from the roots. Another shudder and the smooth orbs of her eyes are wetly reflective, sclera and iris, white and topaz-brown and angry.

"You," I whisper, and red lips part over sharp white teeth, and the noise from her throat is a growl.

I step back, but her perfect hands are around my neck: soft as silk, hard as stone.

ITSY BITSY SPIDER

"COME *ON*, DIANA, this mess has to go."

Diana Rackham has decided by now that her younger sister Pippa is entirely too practical for her own good. She squats over the copper dustpan, which is full of gears and glass shards and bits of wire, and scowls up at Pippa. "No, I'm not throwing it all away, not when some of this is still usable. Now, give me one good reason I shouldn't kill Rowena."

Pippa sighs and shakes her head, the movement jostling the beaded comb fixed in her chestnut hair. "Because she's our sister and she's only seven, and you don't kill a seven-year-old for breaking a clockwork rabbit."

Diana glowers at the remains. Grubby little Rowena had done a bang-up job, no pun intended; the only clue that this twisted-up mess had ever *been* a clockwork rabbit is one forlorn metal ear, once cunningly jointed to twitch realistically. "You do when it cost you two hundred pounds and you made it for her birthday! Besides, Pip, there's breaking it and then there's throwing it at the wall in a fit of pique because she's out of chocolate bears."

Diana picks the undamaged ear from the pile and puts it in her apron pocket. "Anyway. Just sweep that up and take it downstairs, I'm going out to think."

Pippa knows that tone. "Diana, you're not going to do anything to her, surely."

"Why not?" But Diana snorts and waves her away. "All right. No, don't look at me like that, I'm not going to kill Rowena. But my next project's going to be something she'll leave alone."

***

She says that, but Diana gets to Fairweather Park with no clearer idea than that she should have brought a coat or at least a hat; it's late autumn and the brisk air isn't exactly conducive to tramping around in just a shirtwaist and skirt and last year's boots. Still, she came out here to think, so she plunks down on an iron bench to do that, trying to ignore the damp cold that immediately soaks into the backs of her thighs.

Damn Rowena. Oh, Diana loves the filthy little chocolate addict fiercely, despite the fact that she's high-tempered and into everything and always at least slightly dirty. *Mother should have lived to see how she's turning out*, she thinks, *Mother would—*

No. Best not to pursue that line of thought any further. Diana sighs, flicks lint from her skirt and tries again. Rowena loves Diana's clockwork toys, though sometimes it seems her favorite part of them is flinging them against the wall to hear them go smash. The rabbit had hurt especially; cost aside, it had taken Diana nearly three months to build the thing and keep it hidden from those grubby little hands, and she'd even ordered a separate voice-command recognition module to put in so Rowena could talk to the thing. Three years in university to study clockwork engineering, three years of being the only woman in her class, and a perfectly salable project ruined by all that temper over chocolate candy—

Diana stops. The piece of lint is still on her skirt, is in fact picking its way up the fabric. She tugs at her glasses and leans in for a close look: a tiny, tiny green spider, navigating the unfamiliar corduroy terrain like an intrepid eight-legged explorer.

"Rowena would run screaming," she laughs softly, and the thought gives her pause. "That's it. That's *it*. I can build a clockwork spider and she'll never go near it!"

She gets up with a crow of triumph, sending the real spider tumbling. "Oh, I should have thought of it sooner. Now if Pippa just hasn't thrown everything away..."

***

It's taken three hours, but Diana's finally spread everything out on the concrete floor of her little basement laboratory and begun separating it into piles: wire (usable); wire (irrevocably bent past straightening); springs, screws and pins; cogs (broken—how the blazes can a seven-year-old break a cog? Force of will?); cogs (unbroken); mainspring (somehow, thankfully, unscathed) and the small, only slightly battered voice module. The batteries had sprung out, of course, but they'd been just about ready for replacement anyway. The only things that haven't escaped Pippa's cleaning wrath have been the rabbit's brown glass eyes, which had shattered and of course needed sweeping up, and its other ear, a twisted mess of enameled steel and brass filigree.

Diana sits in the midst of her piles and takes the previously rescued ear out of her pocket, stroking it. She lays it in the center of the stash and exhales; she'd been attached to Bunbun, when she admits it, more attached than she'd thought Rowena had been...

"Didi?" That's Pippa, her voice a little muffled by the lab's heavy door. Of course she doesn't knock; she never knocks, just stands at the door and shouts. "Are you in there? Father wants to see you. He's in the study."

"Oh, *hell*," Diana mutters, though she guesses she shouldn't be surprised. She gets up carefully, stepping over the sorted hardware; she'll have to pick up the good bits later so Pippa can sweep up the last of the broken ones. "All right, all right, I'm coming."

***

"I'm sorry about your rabbit."

Grenville Rackham speaks with his back to his eldest daughter, his gaze fixed somewhere out the study's big plate-glass window, maybe on the yellowing trees and wet brown rose bushes and decidedly dead hyacinths. His voice is distant, hollow, and Diana can't remember a time in the past seven years when it hasn't been—or, for that matter, very many times in those same seven years that he's set foot outside this room. Oh, she knows he *does*, he eats and sleeps and bathes, obviously, but every time she sees him, it's here. He's as grey as the dust on the bookshelves; he doesn't come in the dining room. He doesn't even see his accounting clients in person anymore.

"It's not a terrible loss." The words catch in her throat and come out hoarse. "Or even a total one. I've got all the good parts sorted out, I'll build something else."

Grenville turns at that, for a moment, enough for Diana to see a faint knowing gleam in one grey eye and a very slight smile. "But not for Rowena."

"Well, no." Diana brushes down the front of her skirt. "For myself. I—I was thinking a little spider, actually." Now she's said it, she can't stop. "Well, not so little, maybe as big as a tea saucer, with articulated legs and that voice module—"

"Diana." Grenville says it quietly still, finally turns fully to look at her. "Athena would be proud of you. So bright and quick and inventive."

How long since he's even said her mother's name? *She'd be proudest of Rowena,* Diana thinks with a pang; she's going to have to be nicer to her youngest sister. Eventually. Somehow. Maybe when Rowena's thirty. "Thank you, Father."

"She'd be amused by your little clockworks. But mostly she'd be proud." Grenville smiles, for an instant, and beckons her to his desk. "Now sit down and let's work out what your 'little' spider is going to cost me."

***

It's been a good day, Diana reflects, hefting her stack of library books and walking up the front steps. It's been a good month, actually; she's built most of the spider's head, all of the legs are properly articulated, and now—she fumbles with the door—she's just about ready to start on the body—

"Hold it right there." Pippa's pulled the door open and is glaring out at her, one hand clutching the broom and the other firmly on one hip. "If even one of those books is about spiders you can take them all right back."

"Pippa." Diana shifts the books crossly, shoves her glasses up. "Nothing is about spiders."

"Everything is about spiders!" Pippa shouts. "Three weeks! Three weeks of books about spiders and drawings of spiders and even bloody *dinner* conversations about spiders!"

"Pip, your language," Diana says mildly. "It's nothing about spiders. I'm done with that, I've got my designs drawn."

"And you showed them at the table last night and gave Rowena nightmares!" Pippa fumes with all the indignation a seventeen-year-old can muster. "All right, then, what's all this?"

"Wiring and basic chemistry," Diana says flatly; she's not mentioning that one last book on arachnid anatomy, slim and hidden in the midst of the others. "It's been eighteen months since I left university, and six since I built Rowena's rabbit. I want a little refresher before I go further."

"Well, all right." The tone of the words suggests she's gone far enough already, but grudgingly Pippa stands back and lets her come into the foyer. "I still can't believe Father's paying for you to build this—*thing*."

"He pays to keep you in ribbons and dresses," Diana points out. "It's not my fault I'm not so vain. Anyway, another week or so and I'll be finished."

Pippa shudders. "That's what I'm afraid of."

***

Diana sits back on her heels in the middle of the laboratory floor. She's been down here two—or is it three?—days, snatching sleep at the desk, going upstairs only for a call of nature or a quick wash and a change of clothes, just grabbing an apple or a sandwich or a cup of tea before coming back down.

She studies the spider. He's a little larger than a saucer, actually, more the size of a dinner plate. When had she started thinking of him as "he"? The better part of two weeks, easily. "Tocky," she says. "Maybe it's silly but it sounds right. You're going to need a proper name. After all, Rowena's rabbit had one."

Tocky is silent. The spider is inert, lying on the floor with its triple-jointed legs curled beneath its body. She'd got the tiny eye-lights installed today, connected to the same batteries as the voice-recognition module; they light up nicely when their switch is toggled, almost like the spider's round back: a dome of water-tumbled, bottle-green glass she'd bought off a dustman. She'd striped the glass here and there with black enamel for a sort of poisonous look, and ornamented it at the back by a thin wedge of glossy filigreed brass. Diana strokes the metal, thinking that it looks out of place now, and shakes her head. "Sorry," she mutters. "That was the last good piece of Bunbun, I had to do something with it."

She runs a finger over Tocky's mandibles. The tiny fangs are sharp, hollow; she'd made them from the tips of unused hypodermic needles she'd begged from Dr. Lundsford in the next street. That had been one of the trickier parts, hooking the needle fangs to the 'venom' reservoir she'd built in Tocky's abdomen. Not enough to hurt Rowena, of course, but enough of a sting to make her think twice about bothering *this* toy.

"Tomorrow I'll go see Jensen at the pharmacy and get some carbolic acid," she tells the dormant spider. "Then I'll have my very own lab guardian. What's proof against Rowena is proof against damned near anything."

✳✳✳

Getting the carbolic acid in had been easy, though Jensen had been disbelieving when she'd told him of its purpose. On a whim Diana has screwed an eyebolt into Tocky's back below the head, just large enough to fit the clasp of a chain leash. "We'll go for a walk in the morning and he can just see for himself."

At the sound of her voice the spider swivels round; it's been methodically walking the lab floor since she wound it up, tiny pointed metal feet making an almost musical *tiktiktiktik* noise as it walks. Reprogramming the voice-command module to recognize a new name had been difficult—she'd actually had to read the manual—but by four this morning Diana had persevered; damned if she's going to have a spider called Bunbun. "Come, Tocky."

Tocky *tiktiks* its way to her feet, stopping when it nudges her shoes. Diana reaches down and pats it. "Good boy."

There's a knock on the lab door. Diana's first thought is that it's Rowena, and she scowls; she wants to save this particular surprise. But a glance at the clock tells her it's not yet noon, so Rowena should still be at her lessons; another glance downward at her own blouse and skirt tells her she's decently presentable, even if her shoes are dusty. "Come in."

"Diana?" It's her father, wearing his usual look of weariness and half-preoccupation, but undercut with concern. "Are you all right? You've been down here four days."

"Have I? No wonder I feel every one of them," Diana admits; she's ready for a long hot bath and a steak or two. "Oh, I've been coming out at night, having a bite or two, cleaning up." She straightens; her neck feels like it's gained a permanent crook from sleeping at her desk. "But I'm finished, Father, come look."

Grenville steps down the last stair and into the doorway properly. "What have you—oh my *God*."

It's said not so much with displeasure as with sheer surprise. Diana grins and picks up the spider, its jointed legs folding up as contact with the floor is broken. "Do you like him? His name's Tocky."

She holds Tocky out, and her father takes a half-step back. Tentatively he grasps a leg and carefully extends it. "So you're seven again too, naming your stuffed animals? Didi, sometimes I think you get too attached to your little creations."

"Oh, Father, hardly. But if Ro can name her rabbit, I can name my spider." Diana inserts Tocky's winding key and gives it a few good turns, making all the legs extend again, then sets the spider on the floor. "Watch. Tocky, walk."

Tocky picks its way around in a circle, then starts off: *tiktiktiktik*. Grenville's eyebrows go up and Diana's sure she hears her father swear under his breath. "Well," he says at last, "I must say I'm impressed—"

"Rowena!" That's Pippa, shouting from upstairs after the sound of footsteps clambering downwards. "Ro, I don't care if the door's open, you know you're not supposed to go down there!"

"Oh, Rowena!" Diana grins at her father and puts on her very best smile. "Come on down, sweetie, I've got something to show you."

TEMPEST

HE SWIMS OUT to the reef and waits for her, because hell is empty and all the devils are here and he has not yet learned to be afraid.

She comes: bare and white, hair and eyes and skin, flat feet and webbed fingers and thin mouth stretched in a too-toothed smile—

(the sky is lead and the sea is black and she is white save her gills and more secret places, fringed-rich-red, pulsing, waiting)

—and her mouth is too wide for proper kissing but he does it anyway, warm flesh to cold, his hands slotted into hers, short nails pulling at the membranes between her fingers.

She tastes of rain, of salt, of blood: and he has not learned to be afraid—

(he will be found in three days' time, neck broken in three places, bitten through to porcelain shards of spine)

—and when she laughs quicksilvery he tips his head back, baring his throat, stars wheeling briefly overhead in his vision before blanking out, and there is hunger raw in the rows of her teeth but something in her eyes like kindness—

And he is not afraid, because hell is empty.

ZERO HOUR

THE FIRST THING you do when you wake up is peel your eyelids open with your fingers.

Your lashes are gummy, and almost stick together again when you squint against the too-bright light. Your tongue feels parched and furry, clinging to the roof of your mouth, and when you work your jaws there's the distinct sting of flesh parting. You taste something metallic, like blood, but thick and rancid. Sweat slicks your forehead, oily and cold.

Cold. You fumble the back of your hand across your forehead and yes, your skin is cool. Your fever must have broken.

Annalise had been sick at the office party last night, or at least she'd complained of feeling unwell. So had Brian and Tamsin, separately; Brian had said his kids had come home from school aching. Some sort of crud, you'd all agreed, something going around. They'd decided to go home early. You'd felt fine at the time, but talking to them had left a psychosomatic scratchiness in your throat.

Or at least you'd thought it was psychosomatic. By the time you'd pulled into your own driveway, you could feel the swell of your tonsils every time you swallowed, and your skin had felt like parchment paper left in an oven too long, brittle and scorched around the edges. You'd choked down water and ibuprofen in the kitchen, then stumbled out of your stilettos and staggered to the bedroom where, vision blurring and hands beginning to shake, you'd read your temperature on the digital thermometer as a hundred and four.

I'll go to the ER, you'd told yourself dizzily. Right after I just lie here a few minutes.

But that had been last night, or so you think. You're still in the cocktail dress you'd worn to the party, and as you struggle upright, limbs heavy and joints crackling in protest, you catch sight of the bruises in the creases of both your elbows, large and slate-blue. The skin around them is grey, and panic twists heavily in your chest as you scrabble the thermometer from the bedside table and shove it beneath your stiff tongue. In a few seconds the thermometer's alarm shrills, and you pull it free, squinting harder; the skin of your forehead creases and splits with the effort.

Eighty-five degrees.

You can't feel your heartbeat.

Something is very, very wrong.

Standing is difficult; your knees have locked almost completely, nearly pitching you straight forward onto the floor. But you catch yourself against the nightstand and totter into the bathroom, holding onto the fixtures, the furniture, the walls. You grip the edges of the sink and haul yourself in front of the mirror and scream, except you don't. The noise that comes out as you stare at yourself is airless and soft.

The skin of your face is ash grey. Your eyes are sunken and semi-opaque, surrounded by deep purple lids. You pull back your lips and see blackened gums shriveling away from your teeth. Shuddering, you hug yourself and rub your icy forearms, and a flap of skin drops away from one limb like a discarded glove.

Whatever this is, you don't think the ER can help you now.

AND DROWN MELANCHOLY

THE HEADACHE HAS lasted nineteen days.

Nineteen days. Charlotte can count every one of them. It had started the day after she'd spiked her Coke a little too vigorously and stumbled into the pond at the company picnic: an insidious little pressure behind her eyes and above her upper teeth. Sinuses, she'd thought, the consequence of snorting out a noseful of stinking, muddy water. It had taken two days to get the gritty feeling out of her mouth and the eye-watering bouquet of algae and catfish out of her nasal cavities.

By then, she'd realized it wasn't her sinuses.

✳✳✳

Migraine. That's been the consensus, over the last seventeen days, of two general practitioners and a neurologist. Charlotte's inclined to agree with them; she doesn't have the throat-quivering nausea, not yet, but the auras are there, little flecks and zags of color that flit in and out of the edges of her vision like UFOs, eluding her most concentrated efforts to focus on them, jiggling and dancing with every throb between her temples. The pain's there too, rasping at the backs of her eyeballs, thrumming between her teeth, jackhammering the inside of her skull so hard she expects to blow out bone dust with every breath. The doctors' solutions had been bed rest, Tylenol, and time; Charlotte's boss had watched her zombie-shuffle into work, glazed and tight-jawed, right up until yesterday and had suggested a week off instead. That suits Charlotte fine: it lets her sit home in constant dark and slug down the pain with booze and the oxycodone left over from last year's dental surgery. Not the wisest combination, she knows, but it's the only thing yet that's even taken the edge off.

Charlotte lolls in her overstuffed recliner, her third extra-tall double-strength rum and Coke close at hand, waiting for the pill she'd sucked down to kick in. The late-night news program is the only thing she's found that isn't too bright or too loud; she's got the volume low, just enough to pick up, to occupy the one sliver of her brain that isn't threatening to explode from her ears. Even now, at midnight, with all the blinds closed and all the lights off, she can only squint in agony at the screen for a second before giving up and closing her eyes.

"Now for an update. Medical researchers believe they may have found a parasite responsible for the nation's recent outbreak of drowning deaths. Some of the footage you're about to see may be disturbing to some viewers."

Charlotte slits one puffy eye open, then the other. The news anchor is a bottle blonde with a weary gaze, and her voice has pitched up with urgency. Nearly two hundred people have drowned across the country in a month, all of them seemingly accidents, all baffling. There'd been talk about it at the office three weeks ago, when the number had been a few dozen, rumors and jokes about some secret cult urging its members to suicide in pools and bathtubs; she'd even had a few barbs thrown her own way after the pond incident, suggesting she circle her backyard pool with a padlocked fence just in case God or aliens gave her the urge. The scene switches to a bearded bald man, Dr. Something-or-other, wearing a lab coat over his suit in a book-crammed office, and Charlotte tries to focus.

"Surgeons have extracted worms from the brains of some recent victims." His voice is flat with practice, and the scene cuts away, to the shore of a lake. Somewhere in Tennessee, if Charlotte's cramping brain reads the caption right. The voiceover continues: "The specimens haven't yet been positively identified, but there are early signs that they may be a species closely related to *Spinochordodes tellinii*, a hairworm known to cause similar behavior in..."

Charlotte tunes him out. Her gaze is on the scene, eyes open wide now: a man in a green T-shirt and purple shorts lies leaking on the ground, recently dredged up, circled by emergency personnel. His face is a smeared slate blur, the concealing effect growing into a pixelated muddle of bruise tints as the camera zooms in; but the blur doesn't cover the sand, caked like packed brown sugar in his sodden blond hair, or the blackish trail of lumpy blood that has drooled from his left ear. Charlotte stares, momentarily fascinated, as the blood continues to ooze.

"...not yet sure how this animal has evolved to infect humans, or how infestation begins. However, reports from victims' family members suggests symptoms..."

On the screen, someone is shaking out a white sheet over the drowned man's body. The camera shifts away, but not before Charlotte catches sight of a military-style boot, so shiny it reflects the red crawl of the ambulance lights.

"...dizziness, stiffness, lack of coordination... behavioral changes in the presence of water..."

Between the boot and the body, partially obscured, is a long, thin creature that lies coiled in a heap: the unnamed parasitic worm, Charlotte supposes, though it's like nothing she's ever seen. No worm could be this slender, an overcooked strand of brown spaghettini sauced with blood and black flecks. It squirms visibly, and the sight makes her sore brain twinge in sympathy. A blue-gloved hand swoops into the scene, bundling the worm into a clear plastic bag. Charlotte's eyes ache, her vision joggling momentarily. She blinks hard, seeing spots, and drinks off her rum and Coke.

She needs more Coke. Grimacing, Charlotte eases out of the recliner, leftover ice rattling in her glass as she sways. She starts jerkily toward the TV, then remembers she'll need its light to grope her way round the kitchen—thank God for open floor plans when you're too drunk to navigate properly.

At the refrigerator, dull warmth begins at the top of

Charlotte's head and paints its way down the inside of her skull. Her stomach does a little flip and her jaw relaxes; finally, *finally*, the oxycodone has made its appearance and she can forego the rum. She pours her soda with shaking hands, trying not to weep from sheer relief.

Back in her recliner, fresh drink at the ready and television still droning low, Charlotte falls asleep.

***

Charlotte awakens to three realizations.

The first is that there's light seeping through the blinds, cool and grey as though the sun's gone into hiding, and that the television screen is frozen in a garish striped test pattern. Both are still far too bright for her liking, and she scowls as her eyelids snap immediately into the squint she's worn for nearly three weeks. The second is that opening her eyes has roused the pain again, a more frenetic throb than last night, one that vibrates her eardrums and crackles along her jawbone under her teeth; reflexively, she grinds her molars.

The third is that she's madly thirsty.

Charlotte fumbles for the glass of Coke she'd poured up earlier. The tumbler slips through her fingers and she snatches at it, but it thuds on the floor. She sits up, groaning at the stiffness in her neck, and looks over the side of the recliner; the heavy glass is intact, but there's nothing on the carpet beneath it, not a spill, not a droplet, not a fragment of melting ice. She hadn't even sipped at it before she'd fallen asleep, she's mostly positive of that. Now it's empty and she doesn't remember drinking it.

"God." The word comes out thick, and Charlotte gingerly rubs her hands over her face, wincing when she gently prods her eyelids. Her tongue feels glued to the roof of her mouth, prying loose only with effort, slipping over the foul sour-sweetness coating her teeth. Suddenly her thirst is a knot in her gut, twisting and raw. Water. She needs water.

Charlotte gets to her feet clumsily, nearly pitching to the floor as she gropes to pick up her glass. Getting the tumbler in one hand, and holding the back of her head with the other, she totters into the kitchen, away from the rainbow stare of the TV. In the dimness she scrabbles for the tap and swallows saliva. The aura's not elusive now; it streaks her vision, bloody red and dazzling.

Water. Cold. It slops over her hand as she wrestles the glass under the faucet. Her brain squirms in her skull, a live thing all its own, a pulsating mess of knife-edge pain. She drinks with her eyes closed, and the red streaks elongate and snap, turning white, becoming stars that cast off sparks with every swallow. She fills and empties the glass six times, only stopping when her stomach threatens to rebel, but it's not enough.

It's not enough. Her brain is on fire; she can feel the fever slithering through its shell of protective membranes. Her tongue is a swollen sponge, her throat a desert, her skin a withered root aching for moisture. She drops the glass into the sink. More. She needs more.

The pool.

Charlotte lurches toward the sliding doors that open into her backyard. There's a fence—isn't there a fence? No, that was a joke, a joke. She works the lock with graceless hands, frustration welling from her arid throat in a croaking wail, until the door bursts open and she collapses onto the lawn.

Dazed, she lies there a second; it's barely daylight and the grey is comfortable. But the grass is wet and her tormented nerves shriek, *waterwaterwater*. Charlotte drags herself upright, takes three steps toward the pool and falls again, her vision swarming with whirling sparks, pressure building in her skull as though her brain's begging to be let out. A swim. That's all she needs. Just a swim, and she'll feel better.

Weeping, blinded, she begins to crawl.

THE LURE OF LIGHT

NO SERVICE.

Lisa can just make out the tiny words through the spiderweb of cracks that fans out from the upper left corner of her phone screen, a corner that's now jagged and missing pieces of its outer shell. She hadn't meant to throw the damned thing down quite so hard, but after getting seventeen texts from Karen within ninety seconds of arriving at the hotel's front doors, Lisa had just sort of...snapped.

The desk clerk, the sort of good-looking woman Karen might have called *distinguished* or *academic* (but never in Lisa's hearing, not these days), had smirked at her, and almost by compulsion Lisa had found herself kneeling on the rich carpet to search for tiny shards of glass and plastic, trying to mumble an apology. *Sorry about that. I told her I'd made the trip okay. It's just a week, she doesn't have to bug me, it's just a week, I'm sorry, I'm sorry.*

She was, Lisa realized in that moment, getting tired of apologizing.

***

Somehow, Lisa had checked in without further incident, getting her room key without her cheeks bursting into flames from embarrassment or any wayward bits of glass finding their way into her shoes. She'd been surprised to see that the key was an old-fashioned brass one, heavy and tarnished, on a ring that dangled a large steel 8; she'd shoved her fingers through the loops of the numeral, squeezed her broken phone in the other hand, and trudged up the great winding staircase several steps after the frowning old bellhop, who'd handled her two suitcases as if they were a personal affront and hadn't yet offered her more than a tight-lipped grimace—in fact, he'd deposited her bags at the door to her room and turned back to the stairs without even telling her to enjoy her stay.

Odd people. Karen would be saying "I told you so," if she were here now; she'd practically said it as soon as Lisa had found Lake Manor online. *You don't want a place like that, I hear it's haunted and people disappear and it's probably full of weirdos and anyway we can still afford something nice—*

Dammit. Lisa feels a little better now that she's ensconced in her room, her week's worth of clothes hung up in the wardrobe and ten love-worn paperbacks stacked neatly on the dresser in fives, and she's not about to ruin the beginning of a good mood by concentrating on her girlfriend's endless worrying. It's the reason she's here, after all, to get a break; what she'd seen as Karen's cute nervousness at the beginning of their relationship is wearing thin now, four years later, especially since poor student test scores had brought Lisa's first-grade teaching career to an abrupt and apparently permanent halt in May, and then in June Emily—

Lisa closes her eyes and clenches her teeth. For a few seconds she just sits on the edge of the bed, stroking the worn silk comforter to calm herself, bouncing a little against the firmness of the mattress. Then she picks up her phone, wincing as another bit of glass flakes off in her palm, and nudges the screen.

It takes several taps on the fragmented surface before the device flickers to life, but at last Lisa's finally rewarded. Never mind that most of the icons don't seem to respond now; she can still see her wallpaper, her Emily.

Despite the screen cracks, her daughter still looks radiant. It's Lisa's favorite picture, Emily's first day of kindergarten last August. The five-year-old had insisted on a white dress and white shoes, despite Karen's repeated warnings that they'd simply get filthy on the playground. In the shot, Lisa sees her own blonde hair, her own dimples, Emily's ear-to-ear smile adorably gapped by a lost tooth. She can close her eyes tight and still feel that warm little body in her arms, still smell Emily's bubblegum shampoo. Emily had loved kindergarten, and had been over the moon at the thought of having Mommy for her first-grade teacher the next year.

Lisa had been over the moon too, before the budget cuts, before the accident.

It should have been simple: Lisa had been dropped off at the farmer's market, Emily's giggly "Be good, Mommy," still fresh in her ears, while Karen made the trip to the dentist to have Emily relieved of a wiggly front tooth that wasn't coming out on its own. It hadn't been Karen's fault—Lisa knows that, intellectually; Karen wouldn't have *deliberately* got their car plowed through that intersection by that idiot drunk driver—but there have been a lot of times in the past three months that she's caught herself thinking how Karen should have been more careful, more watchful, more *something*, dear God, it's not fair that Emily *died* and Karen walked away without so much as a *scratch*—

Lisa catches her breath. The phone's gone dark, and the unbroken part of the screen is dotted with something. Tears. God, she's lost it again. Swearing under her breath, she sets the phone down at her side and swipes her face with both hands. Even her shirt's wet; she wipes her fingers on it angrily and hopes there's no one in the next room who's overheard her sobs. Lisa stumbles to her feet and toward the bathroom, vision blurred by a fresh wave of moisture. She feels her way to the sink, and splashes icy water across her face and into her eyes, avoiding the bleary reflection in the bathroom's ornate mirror.

When she comes back out, she leans in the doorway, breathing hard, her cheeks stinging from being scrubbed with the tail of her shirt instead of a fluffy hotel towel. So much for her good mood; she needs something to do, to take her mind off Emily *right now*, but her eyes are too sore for reading and neither room service nor the tiny hotel bar sounds the least bit appealing.

A nap. She'll have a nap. No elbow-jostling, no wriggling in discomfort to accommodate an extra body, and when she wakes up, things will be better. They have to.

"It's just a week," she sighs.

***

Mommy?

Lisa bolts upright, nearly falling off the bed; the phone thumps to the floor. "Emily? *Emily?*"

No answer. She glances around wildly and then remembers where she is, heart hammering in her chest. "Oh, Jesus." Lisa pushes sweat-slick hair out of her face and slumps back onto the mattress, grabbing the comforter in her fists, her scalded eyes helplessly leaking tears. "Why can't I keep my shit together? Why did it have to be Emily? Why couldn't it have been fucking Karen?"

The words come out and she stops cold, shoving the knuckles of one hand into her mouth. "Oh, God, I'm sorry," she whispers, rolling over to reach the fallen phone. "I'm so sorry. I love you, Karen. I still love you."

Still apologizing. Lisa sits up, shaking her head to clear it. The light slanting through her room's sole window carries the purple of oncoming twilight—how long has she slept? "You were right," she murmurs, talking to the empty air since her phone's beyond picking up a signal. "I shouldn't have come here like this." Knees creaking as she stands, she goes to the window and pulls at the burgundy velvet drapes, grimacing for a second at the feel of the dusty, heavy fabric against her palm. From here she can see the lake the hotel's named for, shrouded in thick rosy mist; someone's walking along the cobblestone path that leads to the pier and the water's edge, but their features are lost to her in the fog. She drops the velvet panel and turns away, back to the books on the dresser and the clothes in the wardrobe. "I don't care about getting the money back. I'll pack all this up in the morning and come home. I'll find a job. We'll work something out. Somehow."

***

Even after a bath and a change of clothes, Lisa still feels too unsettled to eat. Never mind what Karen had said about haunting; she has enough ghosts of her own. Still, she guesses she needs something in her stomach, so she makes her way back downstairs, receiving a glare from the still-silent bellhop as he ascends with another load of luggage. Apparently she's slept through the arrival of more guests.

Two of those guests are in the hotel's sitting area, across the lobby from the front desk: an elderly woman in a pastel pantsuit and a small girl, red-haired and freckled. Her granddaughter, Lisa supposes, and takes the time to get herself a cup of tepid coffee and a banana nut muffin before looking for a seat. "Hi. You just got here?"

"We did." The woman smiles. "Violet Conroy. You may have passed my Henry on the stairs, trailing that fellow who totes the bags—Henry's very particular about our things." She looks around. "It's a lovely hotel. I adore that staircase—although I'm sure my back won't be so fond. And the gas lighting, that's a nice touch."

Gas lighting? Lisa hasn't noticed—but yes, this entire area is lit with gas lanterns, the flames yellow and flickery and a little creepy. "I'm Lisa," she answers, unwilling to offer more; instead, she turns to the little girl. "You're pretty."

The child laughs, showing a gappy smile. "Go on," Violet urges, "say hello, Emily."

Emily. Lisa swallows her coffee in a hurry; she can practically hear the blood draining from her face. "Excuse me," she chokes, "did you say—"

"Hannah." Violet is tousling the red hair. "Come on, Hannah, don't be shy."

Lisa drinks the rest of her coffee in a hurry, feeling her heart clamber down from her throat. "You know, I just got here a few hours ago myself," she says, grabbing her muffin. "I think it's time to have a good look around."

Jesus, I've got to get out of here.

***

The mist over the lake isn't nearly as picturesque as it had looked online.

She'd heard ducks out here, or something like them, and had sacrificed her muffin without glimpsing anything. Up close, standing as near to the water as she can without losing sight of her toes, Lisa realizes that the haze is flat-white and immensely thick; her skin and clothes feel damp, as though she's walked through a dense fog, but there's none of a fog's shifting wispiness. She stretches out an arm and can't see anything past her elbow. Wiggling her fingers uneasily, Lisa looks back over her shoulder and can just make out the lines of the hotel. She pulls her hand back.

Her phone vibrates in her pocket.

Lisa yelps, stumbling as she tries to pull it out, teetering forward toward the water. *Don't fall in, Mommy, they'll never find you here* snakes through her head and of course it's Emily's voice, why does it have to be Emily's voice, and Lisa yanks the phone free and her knees fold and she sits down hard.

Smarting, breathless from the impact, Lisa clumsily wipes condensation from the screen. Some of it smears around the cracks, but it clears enough that she can read the message.

Be good, MMommy

Lisa cries out, but bites her tongue hurriedly, struggling back to her feet, squeezing the phone in both hands as though she can mend the damage through sheer force of will. Somebody's fucking with her, this has to be a sick joke of some kind—

The message is from her own number.

This isn't possible. Lisa scrubs one hand on her jeans to wipe her eyes as the screen blurs. *There's no way anyone could—Karen? Is Karen doing this?* The idea is ludicrous enough that Lisa snorts, then sniffles heavily. Karen is a worrier, not a prankster. She'd never be cruel enough to do something like this, not when she was the one in the accident.

The phone buzzes weakly as another message pops up.

im wAtching you moMMy

***

Lisa hasn't left the hotel. She hasn't even packed her bags. She's barely left the bed.

It's too soon, that's all. She's rational, she knows this. It's only been three months since Emily died; it had been foolish for Lisa to think she could go halfway across the country to this spot in the dead end of nowhere and be fine by herself. She hasn't grieved enough yet to venture so far; that's why she hears giggles in the empty hallway, and taps on the outside of her window when there's not even a tree branch nearby, and *Mommy* in every creak of the floorboards. It's purely psychological.

But *I hear it's haunted*, Karen had said, and that's why Lisa won't look in the bathroom mirror, afraid of just whose face she'll see.

The phone lies beside her on the bed, within easy reach. She can see through the cracks well enough to see that the battery indicator's in the red, but she has no clue what will happen if she tries to charge it. She'd rather be a grief-crazed mother than the idiot who makes the news by burning down the hotel.

It vibrates. She grabs it.

i lovve you mommY

Lisa slams the phone screen-down onto the comforter and curls up in a tight knot to sob.

***

The impact is soundless, a sudden wild careening through traffic and the crunch of the right front headlight into a utility pole. Karen's airbag deploys. Lisa's face bounces off the back of the front seat's headrest and her mouth begins to sting. Wait, hadn't she been at the market? Why is she still in the car? "Karen?" she asks thickly, but gets no answer.

Karen's not in the car. Lisa yanks at her door handle, but the door's jammed and won't open. She scrabbles at her seat belt buckle, but it, too, refuses to yield. "Karen?" Lisa screams through mushy lips; cars whiz by outside, frighteningly close. "Dammit, Karen, get me out of this!"

"Mommy?"

"Emily, hold on." Lisa gives up on her seat belt and reaches for her daughter. "Oh my God, Emily!"

Emily's wearing the same white dress she'd picked for the first day of kindergarten, blood spotting the fabric where it's dripped from her mouth, a bag of hand-picked tomatoes spilled across her lap. Her lips are sticky and red, her eyes blank, her head hanging at an unnatural angle. "Emily!" Lisa shrieks again, and this time she spots Karen: standing outside the driver's door with someone in a uniform, laughing. Laughing. Joking. "Karen, goddammit, help us!"

Only laughter reaches her, becoming a golden giggle from the child slumped broken beside her. Then Emily says "Mommy," again, and her head turns with a sick wet grating noise on her fractured neck, and her eyes have the lambent yellowness of the lights in the hotel hallways, and her smile is a ghastly crimson grin with gaps in it. Blood bubbles out where a tooth should have been.

"Dance with me, Mommy."

✳✳✳

In the bathroom, Lisa has to hold on to the sides of the sink to stay upright, but she manages to rinse her mouth—which twinges oddly—and rinse her face with the coldest water she can stand.

She does not look in the mirror.

She draws a cold bath as well, intent on rinsing away this sick sweaty feeling. Afterward, she stands on the bath mat and drips, trying not to think of the sound of the blood spattering from Emily's mouth. "Bad enough I've lost my daughter and my job," she mutters, "and when I get home I may not have a girlfriend either, but my mind? Am I losing my mind?"

She can hear her phone vibrating in the next room.

She towels off and dresses hurriedly.

***

There's not another message.

Annoyed, increasingly uneasy, Lisa turns to her books. She'd picked these ten because they're old favorites, read and re-read and memorized, but she can't concentrate; every time she scans a line she sees the blood on that white dress, on those precious lips. The way Emily's gaze had been frozen, the way her head and neck had been so *strangely* twisted.

That was exactly how she'd looked in the hospital morgue.

Words blur and run on the pages, skimmed blindly, as one book is laid aside for another. By the time Lisa gives up on the distraction, her two neat stacks of five on the dresser are a jumbled, wept-over pile on the floor.

She pushes off the bed, rubbing the back of her neck. The room is almost dark—it's later than she'd realized—but the last light of evening streams in the window with an odd yellow color, shifting between light and dark as though the sun is trapped in a swift churning cloud. The flickering is unpleasant to look at, and Lisa is just reaching to close the drapes when she spots the first movement.

There's another person down at the lake's edge—no, two—no, several. They sway and writhe and she can't quite count them, no matter how hard she concentrates; there seems to always be one more, just at the corner of her vision, and every one of them glows yellow.

It's a trick of the light, it has to be; but Lisa rubs her eyes until they run, and the yellow people are still there, wavering like candle flames about to go out. They shine like the gas lights in the hallway, and as she watches them join hands and begin to dance in a circle, she realizes that the mist shrouding the lake has almost the same creamy radiance.

Lisa looks away again. "Guess I've found the hotel ghosts after all," she says to herself, but when she turns back to the scene, the people are still there, still dancing, glowing brighter now. There's a smaller figure in the center of their circle; it looks up, sees Lisa, and waves.

It's Emily.

Her phone makes a weak noise. Her hands start to shake.

***

i see yoU momMY you cAnt HIde come danCE with MEe

***

When Lisa steps off the cobbled walkway, shivering in the thin white nightgown she'd yanked on because it reminds her of Emily's white dress, the circle of people is still there, and Emily is still in the center.

She can't see her feet, and forces herself to walk. The others let her pass, though walking through the ring is unnerving. They're all stringy-haired and slack-mouthed, faces gelatinous, bodies bloated, eyes staring; they look...*drowned.*

Except for Emily.

As soon as Lisa has breached the circle, Emily runs to her mother and leaps into her arms. "Mommy, you came! I knew you'd come. I watched you."

The words are soft around the edges. Something's wrong; Emily is solid in Lisa's arms, but it's a tenuous solidity, as though the little girl's body might slip into pieces at any moment. Blood streams freely from Emily's mouth, down Lisa's nightgown, filling her nostrils with the scent of wet decay. Lisa retches and coughs, struggling—"Honey, let Mommy put you down, please let

Mommy put you down"—and as the drowned shuffle closer, Emily kisses her mother on the lips.

Blood. Blood and mud and scummy stagnant water, and Emily's rosebud lips are sticky, clinging no matter how Lisa tries to pull away. The others are a tight circle around the pair, and when Emily's small body shakes, disgorging into her mother's throat a stream of bloody liquid rot, Lisa screams and backs away.

But there's no way to go back, only forward, trapped by the insistent press of unstable bodies, and Lisa keeps screaming until she's swallowed by the mist.

***

Of course, no one heard any screams. Douglas Turner doesn't even know the woman's name. All the lawman has to go on is a badly broken smartphone, its screen a mess of sand-filled cracks and its battery dead. Still, if the woman has family, they need to be notified. Maybe someone in his chain of command can get it working.

He drops the dead phone in his pocket. The mist shifts and thins as though it's about to dissipate, as though the sun's about to burn it away and make it reveal its secrets; and Turner casts his gaze across the water, waiting, waiting.

In all his years in law enforcement, Turner has learned that where Lake Manor's concerned, no one ever hears much of anything.

LITTLE REAPER

ON THE STREET where Death lives, there are no trick-or-treaters.

Not that Death minds. It's a quiet cul-de-sac these days, populated by single middle-aged professionals and elderly couples whose grandchildren only visit infrequently, where the only indiscretions are the ones left on the lawn by a neighbor's dog. Around here, he can practically walk to work every day.

No kids, no teenagers, no police calls for meth labs or midnight shouting matches, and no little candy-grubbing costumed visitors on Halloween.

Oh, Halloween. Death sits back in his recliner, watching SportsCenter with the sound off, and smiles his long-toothed skeleton's grin. Visitors or not, it's the one day he doesn't have to wear a mortal-seeming glamour, the one day he can go around in the cowled 'Grim Reaper' attire he's molded from the thoughts and fears of his neighbors, and nobody asks questions. Mr. Reaper is a good neighbor who keeps his leaves raked and his grass trimmed; the other residents on the street will turn a blind eye to the ghoulish appearance, and to the cobwebs and jack o' lanterns that appear on the front porch. He's allowed to be eccentric for one day.

(Mr. Reaper. He's tried telling them all that his first name is McCormick, but no one ever gets the joke.)

At nine PM, Death turns the TV off. He has an appointment with Mrs. Collins next door at eleven, and needs to sharpen his scythe. He admits he'll miss the tea and cake, and her admiration for his perfectly-cut lawn, but the work has to go on.

At nine-fifteen, there's a knock on the door.

It gives Death pause. Has someone taken the jack o' lanterns as an invitation? Did he leave the porch light on? Is there even candy in the house?

(There is, of course. Living among mortals has given him a weakness for chocolate. He goes into the kitchen just in time to hear a second knock, fetches a Snickers bar from the fridge, and slips it into a pocket of his robe. Wonderful mortal invention, pockets.)

Then Death opens the front door and stares down at himself.

The costume's not an exact likeness. The robe has the slick look of thin polyester, and the blade of the scythe is almost certainly shiny plastic. But the face is arresting: a perfect age-yellowed grinning skull, surrounded by wispy brittle blonde curls that spill out around the black cowl.

A little female Death. He's slightly taken aback. "Hello," he says, but she doesn't answer. Instead she shoves her plastic pumpkin-shaped bucket under his nonexistent nose and shakes it. The contents rattle. Death looks down in the glow of the porch light. The little round pail is full of small, flattish white objects.

Bones. He looks closer. Teeth. Teeth and bones, canines and carpals, premolars and phalanges, some bits with flesh still attached, some twinkling with pockets of silver amalgam. Then she taps the blade of her toy scythe against her wrist; she's wearing a wristwatch, and the sound of blade touching crystal is the clink of steel on glass. The little scythe has begun to glow.

Abruptly, Death understands. "It's time."

She pulls the bucket away and nods vehemently, two hard up-and-down bobs of her head.

Death considers. He's always known this day would come eventually; even avatars of mortality have their limits. Still, he's become selfishly attached enough to the trappings of the living that he hedges, fumbling in his pocket. "Would you like a candy bar? I promise it's not fun-sized."

Skulls are inflexible, as a rule, but the girl cocks her head and squints, then nods again, the same two firm motions. Death reaches out to ease the Snickers into her bucket. He touches the teeth and bones inside, and two of his distal phalanges fall off into the pile. The dissolution's already started.

Death pulls away before he loses any more. She sets the bucket down primly, and shifts her grip on the glowing scythe. It's longer now, taller. So is she.

"Wait," he says.

She watches, silent, expectant.

He gestures around them, at the other houses. "They're kind sorts, for mortals. Give them kindness back. And keep the grass neat."

Another headtilt as she considers. Then she nods again.

"Very well." Death looks down at his small replacement. She'll grow into it quickly; he had. "Go ahead."

The scythe lifts, lazily, and swings, and in its wake there's only a faint shimmer in empty air.

Death pushes her cowl back, shakes her curls loose, and picks up her bucket. She steps across the threshold into the house. Tomorrow she'll have a word with the neighbors about their pitiful lack of Halloween decorations. They'll have to do better next year. But first, there's that appointment with Mrs. Collins. If she hurries, there's time to bake a cake.

Miss Reaper's a good neighbor. It's the least she can do.

HATTIE'S GHOSTS

A PUMPKIN. SHE'S a high school freshman, and her social studies project is to carve a freaking pumpkin.

Elaine hunches her shoulders into the wind. She should have been home from school half an hour ago, and her black zip-up hoodie is far too warm for Tennessee in mid-October, but she doesn't care about either. She hadn't asked her dad to take a job in this backwater and uproot her from everything, and the weather matches her mood perfectly: seething. Her teacher, Mrs. Leventhal, had described it as a 'lighthearted' project to take the class into fall break, but to Elaine it's a stupid idea, made more ridiculous by how desperately she wants to succeed at it.

When she gets to the corner, she pulls out her phone. Three forty-five. She should be at home trying to pull dinner together—*again*—but she wants to grab a pumpkin somewhere and get this project started, even if she's got to trudge all the way back across town to Piggly Wiggly.

Elaine stands by the stop sign and looks around, twisting a length of her inky hair around one finger. The street splits here: potholed pavement heading east into the center of town, red gravel heading west into God knows what.

Something flickers in the wind, catching her eye. It's a cardboard sign across the street, fastened to a tree just where the pavement yields to the gravel; it bears a crooked hand-drawn arrow pointing west, and big unsteadily-printed letters reading GOSTS ı HAF MILE.

Gosts. Elaine squints and mouths the word. A bit of gravel crunches under her boots. Is that supposed to be *ghosts*? It must be some hick with one of those dumb haunted barns, she decides, but she doesn't want to go home yet. She checks her phone again: three fifty-three. Her dad won't be home until after five, and maybe it'll be something interesting. God knows there's nothing else around here.

She clutches her backpack. It's only half a mile.

***

The trek takes her out of town toward a wooded area, past fields of tattered corn stalks and wheat stubble burned into brown smudges. She's a decently fast walker even with her backpack, and after ten minutes, sweaty and mascara-stained, she comes up on a small, weathered farmhouse edged by brown-leaved maple trees that blur into the woods. There's a rickety split-rail fence surrounding it, a rusty mailbox, a bright blue tarp over part of the roof. A lone chicken pecks in the gravel at the edge of the lot.

And the yard is full of pumpkins.

Elaine stares, 'ghosts' momentarily forgotten. She'd never seen a pumpkin patch growing up in New Jersey. There must be dozens in the carefully planted plots in front of the house—creamy orange and round as basketballs, releasing an earthy sweet scent into the sun-warmed air.

"Wow." In spite of herself, she's impressed. She sets her pack down—carefully this time—and unzips it, fumbling in the inner pocket for the little cash she's got on hand. Four dollars—no, six, she'd skipped the cafeteria slop again. *That's enough, right? Surely it's enough for one that's not too big.*

"You need somethin', li'l missy?"

Elaine wads the cash up in her fist. An old woman in a shapeless blue dress and patched half-apron is at her elbow, grinning like a skull, eyes clear green and flinty. Elaine hasn't heard a door open; the woman's been in the yard all along. A German Shepherd trails behind her, bristling but silent, gray-muzzled with age.

"Um." Elaine clears her throat. "Yeah. I need a pumpkin. For school. You know, to carve. Do you sell these?"

"Mmm. You ain't from here." The woman eyes her with the distrust Elaine's grown accustomed to seeing, but nods gruffly. "Carvers're up this way."

She walks toward the house. Elaine follows uneasily, looking around. The pumpkins growing in the plots near the house are a little larger than the ones she'd first spotted, their orange hue starker, and there's no hint of sweetness here. Instead, the odor in the air is meaty and faintly rancid, like cooked beef gone just a bit off. She wrinkles her nose, then catches a whiff of smoke and tracks it to a fire pit not far from the porch, overhung by an enormous black iron pot that's the source of the smell.

She's a witch, Elaine thinks and chokes back a sudden giggle. *No, that's kid stuff. Just some old lady cooking outside because she's too poor to have air conditioning.* She shifts her attention back to the pumpkins. "How much are they?"

"Fifty cents a pound. Dollar a pound for them pie-makers you was eyeballin' back yonder." The woman coughs and spits into the dirt. "I'll go get the scales while you're pickin'."

"Wait," Elaine says. "Do you know anything about some ghosts? I saw a sign—"

"Hah!" The woman laughs, and it's an unpleasant sound. "Seen my sign, did you? My special ones, them are. My Ghosts." The capital letter is practically audible. "I hope you brung more money, li'l missy, them's five dollar a pound."

"Five dollars a *pound*?" Elaine blinks. "Pumpkins? Ghosts are pumpkins? Why the hell would they cost so much?"

She catches herself too late and shuts her mouth so fast her teeth click, but the old woman just responds to the profanity with another cough and another ghastly grin. "Growed special. Come on around behind the house, I reckon you can look."

Elaine hesitates. She only has six dollars, and a one-pound pumpkin won't be big enough to carve properly. Still, she can satisfy her curiosity. "Okay."

She lets herself be led, lifting her feet when she's told—"Mind them roots, ol' oak stump under the grass here"—and finding that the old woman's more nimble than she looks. Rounding the house, Elaine sees a yard that's mostly bare dirt, crossed by the fallen trunk of a lightning-scarred maple. She only sees the pumpkins when she's walked past the tiny slumped back porch into a solitary grassy patch.

Elaine gapes. "They're solid white!"

The old woman cackles and rakes her gray hair up wild. "Surely! Ain't that somethin'!"

Elaine squats at the edge of the grass. There aren't many pumpkins here, but they're just as full and hefty as their orange brethren, and pale as fresh snow. She touches the nearest one: warm, despite lying in the shadow of the house. The rind has a peculiarly leathery texture, and she could swear the supple vines have a pink tinge. "How do you grow them like this?"

"Aw, pumpkins come whitish natural," is the drawled reply. "Started these from seed, got 'em to grow seedless now. It's all in what you feed 'em, that's their supper I got stewin' in the front yard."

Elaine's not listening; she's too busy seeing a perfect blank canvas in her mind. She's got to have one of these, cost be damned.

She jumps up and dusts herself off. "You're right. I don't have enough money yet. But I'll be back, so don't sell any of these till I get one. I want to be first."

The old woman just smiles.

***

She gets home to find her dad's beaten her there.

Elaine groans at the sight of his car in the driveway and dredges up her phone: four-fifty. He's never home from the agricultural extension office before five-fifteen. Taking a deep breath, she mounts the steps and drops her backpack inside the open doorway of the screened-in porch. As soon as she walks into the house, she can smell vegetable soup.

"Dad? Dad, what gives?"

"I'm in here," he calls from the kitchen. He's standing over the stove making grilled cheese sandwiches—the kind, she notices a little guiltily, with too much butter and no crust. The perfect ones, with a pot of veggie soup bubbling on the next burner. "Lainey," he says, sighing, "where have you been?"

She bristles a little at the nickname. "I went walking. It's been a rough day."

He flips a sandwich. "Fifteen-year-old girls shouldn't have rough days."

Elaine sinks into a chair at the kitchen table and pillows her head on her arms. *Fifteen-year-old girls shouldn't have mothers who've been dead five months, or fathers who wither and hide.* She studies her father's profile, the lines around his mouth and the gray in his hair that weren't there before her mom's car crash.

I miss Mom too, she wants to say, though she bites her tongue. It's a taboo subject. Instead, she fiddles with the skull-shaped zipper tab on her hoodie. "Um, look. I need a little money for a school project."

Her father's not frowning yet, but she can see it starting in his eyes long before it reaches his face. "What kind of project?"

"For social studies. I have to carve a pumpkin." Elaine looks up hopefully. "I only have a week."

"For social studies," her father repeats dully. "Why—no, never mind. Fine. We'll go to Kroger this week and get one."

"Dad, no." She pushes back from the table. "I found a place outside town that sells white ones. I want a white one."

He's pulling soup bowls from the cabinet. "You went out to Hattie McClain's place? I can't even get you out of your room in the morning!"

"*Dad*," Elaine grumbles. "It's not far and it's important! This is for school and it's my chance to prove I'm more than just the dumb new girl!"

"Lainey—"

"It's been two months, Dad! Two months and to these hicks I'm still just the 'weird' one." She makes finger quotes around the word. "My mom's dead, my dad's a Yankee, I'm a 'vampire' with a funny accent—"

"Elaine." He plunks a bowl down in front of her. Soup droplets bounce out onto the tabletop. "I'm not talking about this right now." His voice has gone cold and flat. "We'll see about your project later. Not right now."

He drops a spoon beside her bowl. "Now eat and go clean up and do your homework."

***

Elaine has geometry to do, but she's pushed that aside. She can't concentrate on it now.

We'll see. Of all the answers her dad could have given, it had to be the one that means 'no' without making him actually say it. It's practically the only way he's responded to her requests since June. Allowance? We'll see, no matter how many chores she's done or meals she's cooked. School supplies? We'll see. Jesus, she only got clothes for the start of the new school year because her Aunt Tina had taken her shopping before they'd left Jersey for this podunk.

She sits down at her desk and thumbs her phone. One email to Aunt Tina and within an hour, she'd probably have more money than she needs sitting in her PayPal account, but there'd also be a phone call to her dad about why he's not providing properly, and Elaine doesn't want to deal with that right now. Besides, she's pretty sure this Hattie McClain doesn't take PayPal.

She drums her fingers on the desktop, over the notes she's made for her pumpkin. Cut out the top and scoop out the goo. Cut out angled eyes, lowered brows, a mouthful of jagged teeth. Cut drawings into the topmost layer of the rind—crooked houses, leafless twitchy trees, arch-backed cats. Rub powdered charcoal into the lines and wipe the excess off. It'll look awesome. She's Googled it all. The only thing she needs now is the pumpkin, which takes money, and with the mood her dad's been in, she'll probably have to steal the damned thing.

Elaine's drumming stops. She's never done that before. Sneaking out, of course, just to be alone with her thoughts; her dad never comes into her room even to say goodnight, and this rinky-dink town is so quiet, she knows she's perfectly safe. But not stealing. For a pumpkin. A fucking pumpkin.

The thought makes her giggle, but not for long. There's no way she'll pry fifteen or twenty bucks out of her dad for a white pumpkin, not when he'll argue she can buy an orange one for three dollars at Kroger and paint it. And those white pumpkins have such soft, flabby stems—her fingers twitch, recalling the oddness of it—that she's positive her craft scissors will do the job. Her scissors, a small flashlight, the compass on her phone. That should be enough.

She'll need her hoodie, her boots, and her black sweatpants to keep from being seen. This is a single-story house, so there's no climbing down from the window, and since her dad always goes to work and leaves her alone to walk to school, she can sneak out and grab a pumpkin, sneak it back in and carve it, and get it to Mrs. Leventhal with no trouble at all.

No one will even notice she's gone.

***

Elaine shivers despite her too-warm clothes. Having so many stars overhead when she looks up is dizzying, but using the flashlight to keep from stumbling over a lump of fresh roadkill makes her feel too visible. Except for brief snatches to check her phone, she's made the trek by sheer memory. Her calves ache.

Elaine leans on Hattie McClain's fence for a moment to catch her breath, then begins to pick her way through the front yard.

The woman's got a porch light on, yellow and dim, and all the windows are dark. Even so, Elaine shies away from the house as much as she can until she reaches the back. The tiny patch of white pumpkins is visible even by mere starlight.

The one she'd picked out earlier is still here; Elaine recognizes the shape. She squats in the grass, as she had before, and nausea hits almost immediately. The weird meaty smell from before is suddenly all around her, only now it's shit and blood and spoilage, magnified by the day's heat seeping from the ground. Flies buzz, and something squelches under her feet. She pinches her nose shut with one hand and turns on her flashlight with the other. The pumpkins are swimming in a stew of rotten meat, moldy scraps, and thick pink liquid. The patch looks like a crime scene.

Elaine gags and spits, breathing through her mouth as she lets go of her nose and fumbles out the scissors. She'll have to work fast.

She gasps in air and grabs the pumpkin stem, but it feels different now—thicker, almost veiny. She squeezes gently and gets the impression it's full of liquid. Wincing, she finds a thin spot in the stem and slips the scissors around it. Another squeeze, and the stem tears with a ripping sound, fluid gushing over her hands.

Elaine yelps and jumps to her feet, dropping the scissors. Her boots are covered in liquid stench. She vomits helplessly and stumbles back.

Something explodes beside her.

It's the back door, slammed open against the house. Before she can gather strength to run, Elaine is pinned in place by a powerful flashlight beam and the muzzle of a double-barreled shotgun shoved into her belly. Hattie McClain leans over her, looking enormous in her wrath.

"Well. Li'l missy. Out-o'-towner," the old woman growls, jabbing her with the gun. "I reckon you thought you'd make off with one o' my babies."

"Please." Elaine's voice squeaks. "Please don't shoot me."

"Why not? You think you can hurt one o' my babies without

me knowin' it, when I feed 'em from my own hands? You think they ain't gonna cry for me?"

"You're crazy." Elaine sobs, which gets her a harder jab. "*Please!* Just—please let me go! Let me go home and I swear I'll never bother you again! I'm sorry!"

"Sorry, all right." Hattie grunts. "Get your ass in the house 'fore I blow it off."

Elaine stares. "What?"

The shotgun gets lowered, but only for Hattie to tuck it under her other arm and seize Elaine's collar. "In the house," she repeats. "You're gonna feed my babies."

FLYCATCHER

JOLENE CAN'T STOP staring at Sissy's scars.

At least, she assumes they're scars: four pink half-circle indents in the middle of Sissy's forehead, like the marks left by dug-in fingernails. And Jolene knows she's being rude, that it's horrible of her, but she can't stop, no matter how bad she feels or how much she tells herself to look away.

When she'd come back to town yesterday, ten years after high school, Jolene had expected something different for her one-time friend. A little house with a neat yard and a white picket fence, maybe. A job as a teacher, or editor of the town paper; Sissy had always been smart that way. A husband somewhere, at the very least, since Sissy had easily been the most reserved girl in school, the one who blushed brick-red at the dirty jokes told in the lunch line.

But not this. Not a seat in a beat-up rocking chair in a saggy rusting trailer on the outskirts of town, with grimy windows and pressboard walls, sweltering under a lazy ceiling fan. Not Sissy herself, now thin and wan and as blushless as if she's been bled. And certainly not Sissy's one-year-old son Jimmy, crab-creeping strangely across the dirty floor on all fours, who's been the subject of Jolene's gaze almost as much as his mother's marred forehead.

But if Sissy notices the stare, she doesn't let on. Just drones on about her ex Tyler, Jimmy's daddy, whom Jolene barely remembers except as a skinny wispy-bearded boy who'd sucked at playing baseball. About Tyler's meth habit and how she thinks it's the cause of Jimmy's condition, and how the doctors at Vanderbilt think so too, though Sissy's granny always claims it's from that brown recluse that bit Sissy in her second trimester, and really, Tyler could've been a good daddy if he hadn't blown himself to hell shake-and-baking crank in his mama's toolshed, and—

Jolene's broken out of her daze by little limbs clamping around her neck; Jimmy is so light she hadn't even noticed him clambering into her lap. But his laugh is gurgling and bright, and it makes Sissy stop talking and smile, the first real emotion that's touched her bloodless face in an hour.

"How 'bout that," she says, pulling up out of her worn recliner and clapping her hands. "He's awful shy of strangers, but I shoulda known he'd take to you, Jo. You just hold him an' let me find my phone."

Jimmy crows as Sissy leaves the room, and nuzzles wetly into Jolene's neck. His little body is stiff and Jolene embraces him awkwardly, dragging her fingers over his thick blond hair. He smells of sour milk and rot, and Jolene finds herself wondering if this trailer had been Tyler's meth lab. If he'd worn some kind of rings that would account for Sissy's scars.

Then Jimmy sinks his teeth into her neck.

Jolene's shout is strangled. The baby's grip is strong, and she can feel her skin parting for his teeth, for the deep burn of the bite. Then the pain passes, and she realizes something's leaking into her from his mouth, something that stings at first but leaves numbness behind. Spots waver in her vision, but she can't blink them away. She can't blink at all.

"That's enough, now." Sissy lifts Jimmy from Jolene's lap and sets him back on the floor. Jolene tries to look up at her, tries to speak, but her eyes won't move and words won't come, not even when Sissy puts too many hands under her chin and jerks her head up hard enough to make her neck crack.

"I'm sorry it's you, Jo." The curved lines on Sissy's forehead flare more deeply red and then blink open, staring back, one after the other. "But I am glad you came by. We ain't had a visitor in a while, an' Jimmy was gettin' awful hungry."

ASHES

I OPEN MY EYES.

The floor is icy; that's the first thing I notice. The flagstones are freezing, a leaching cold, and I can feel the warmth of my body seeping into the granite underneath me, though the temperature of the surface itself doesn't seem to change.

The quiet encroaches on my mind. My breath rasps in my ears, seconded only by the thud of my heartbeat. I'd performed the summoning ritual perfectly. Whatever I'd called out of the void should still be bound here, waiting my command, breathing, gibbering, something *audible*. Silence is never a good sign.

I try to push myself up. Can I? The stone under my back is a gravity well pulling at my skin, but I strain, getting my shoulders off the floor. The air smells of ash and smoke from burning flesh, and my stomach twists. A knot of pressure rises in my throat. I drop back, turn my head to the side, and open my jaws to let out the flow. I spit when I'm empty and sit up fully at last, weak but mobile. A final trickle slides from my lips, down my shirtfront.

I spare the liquid staining my shirt a glance. It's black. I keep my eyes on the blotch for a second before I finally look down at my forearms, at the markings there. The glyphs should have faded before I was awake; they've always faded before, when I've tinkered in the void, but now they cover my skin in neat perfect rows, as if they've been painted on. They're black too. I rub my left thumb over my right forearm, but the marks don't smear. I'm not imagining them, and the realization makes my gut wrench again. This is new. A message? A warning? I can't read them this time. The knot tightens, rises toward my throat.

I stand unsteadily, wishing I had someone to prop me up. Nothing happens, yet the thought alone should have been enough to bring the creature I'd called forth to my side. I take a few tottery steps out of the quartered and rune-inscribed glyph I'd long ago etched into the basement floor. I turn back to see the smeared summoning circle, the scattered ash and salt, for the first time.

It isn't just broken; it's empty. I don't know what I've pulled from the void—I never know until I see it—but it's gone. It's loose.

I limp up the basement steps, lay my hand on the knob. It rattles in my grasp, the door bowing outward. Claws scrape wood in a rising tone.

On the other side, something growls.

SHOWROOM

ELISE HASN'T BEEN back to the old factory since the disappearances.

She's never known what was made here; the gates were shuttered before she was born. But by her twelfth birthday the fence had been breached, and it's been a late-night hangout ever since: a place to blast the music parents have forbidden, to smoke cigarettes and weed, to drink beer and have sex and try out fledgling spells copied out carefully in spiral-spined Lisa Frank notebooks in purple glitter ink, protection against grounding or failing grades or unfaithful boyfriends.

Most of those hadn't worked, though Elise has heard that Molly Tibbetts' fiancé caught a weird rash one night.

Elise, though. Elise has always preferred to come here in daylight, on Saturday mornings, while her mom's at work and her dad's laid up drunk on the couch in front of some football game. To sit with her legs dangling over the edge of that huge, stained, empty rectangular pool taking up half the floor (what had filled it? Water? Chemicals? Blood? Elise likes to think it was blood), or sketch the graffiti and the rusted-out machine hulks, the patterns cast on the concrete by light streaming through broken and filthy windows. To think. To read. To be.

Then Mary Haskins had come here one night to meet her boyfriend, but had never come home. The same thing had happened with Sonia Smythe. Gabi Franks and Daniella Ramirez had come here for a party. Chalina Ramirez had followed, looking for her sister.

None of them have been seen since. Not so much as a dropped scrunchie or lipstick-stained Solo cup. The gap in the fence isn't mended, but since all the searches have come up empty, the doors have been chained and padlocked shut.

Which does not, Elise has just realized, mean there's no way in. One rear door has been missed. It's locked, but that's nothing, not when she can carefully punch the glass out of its tiny window with a rock and painfully scrape her arm through the opening to reach the inner latch and let herself in. The air in the old building is stale and musty and seems to coat her tongue; it's like the smell in the reptile house at the zoo.

Elise covers her nose with one sleeve. She has to see. She has to know if she'll find anything—and as soon as her eyes adjust, she does.

The empty pool has been filled. Water rocks gently beneath some unfelt breeze, reflecting the white cloud-puffs in the sharp blue sky outside, casting flickering caustics on the walls and floor.

And the statues. The statues are new.

There are half a dozen, maybe more, ringing the edges of the pool, facing it. All female; all standing.

"Weird," Elise mutters, coughing into her sleeve, and approaches the nearest one. None of this has gotten here on its own. Some creepy artist type must have moved in after the teenagers stopped coming. Maybe that's why that back door was accessible. She steps lightly, wishing she hadn't dropped the rock.

But she walks up to the first statue regardless, her own creative curiosity getting the best of her. The hair is pitch-perfect, every strand in place. The clothing folds are realistic enough to seem pliable. Even the crookedly-laced shoe adorning one slightly pigeon-toed foot looks like it was taken from life.

Then Elise recognizes Mary Haskins' face, and screams.

The cry echoes. Elise freezes, but in the split second before the noise dies, she glances around at the other statues, the other faces.

Sonia. Gabi. Daniella. Chalina. There are others Elise doesn't recognize, but her friends are all here, as still as she is, their eyes wide with terror so exquisitely carved that even Chalina's tears have been captured.

"What is this?" Elise mutters, and behind her, something moves.

She doesn't recognize the sound at first; she clenches her fists and holds her own tears at bay. But then it comes closer, and with it a thickening of the reptilian musk, and Elise remembers being thirteen and finding a snake in the garage, how it had smelled, how its scales had whispered on the concrete as it moved. A hand touches the back of her neck, cool and scaled.

We're all here, Elise thinks, *we're all here now*, and she turns around.

SEEING SHADOWS

I STILL REMEMBER the first time I saw one.

I couldn't have been more than six, maybe seven. It was my first day out of school for the summer and my granny was dying in our second upstairs bedroom.

I wasn't supposed to be in there. She'd taken sick the night before and Mama, knowing what was coming, had banished me to the back yard to play all day while she and Daddy and Mama's brother, my Uncle John Ray, hovered around Granny's deathbed and talked in whispers. I didn't know why they were so quiet or what the faint, funny smell was that hung all in the house, but a boy can only play by himself so long, and after a while I just came back inside.

I could hear Granny breathing before I got to the foot of the stairs: start and stop, start and stop, a rattly sound that carried. Somebody was crying. I think it was Daddy.

I'd crept out of bed enough at night to know where the stairs didn't creak. I went up and peeked in the door. Mama stood to one side of the bed, reaching down to stroke the wisps of gray hair back from Granny's forehead. Daddy sat in a straight chair on the other side with Uncle John Ray standing beside him, wedged into the corner with his hands tucked into his armpits. Granny was turning ashen, skin stretched right across her cheekbones, breathing hard and fast.

She took in a shuddery breath and let it out slow, and I saw the shadow.

At least it looked like a shadow. It worked out of her mouth, out of her nose, a cloud of black particles like dust. It slid out of her with that last breath, trailing ragged streamers, and I screamed.

Uncle John Ray swore. Daddy bent over in his chair with his face in his hands. Mama ran to me and swept me into her arms and pressed me into her.

"Hush, Jimmy Earl. Hush, Jimmy Earl. Hush."

The black cloud swirled up to the ceiling and disappeared. I kept screaming. They hadn't seen it.

***

In the middle of August, Uncle John Ray took heat stroke out in the cotton field.

He was muttering and twitching when Daddy wrestled him into the house and onto the couch. Froth flecked his lips. Mama yelled at me to go get cold water; she and Daddy got John Ray out of his clothes and half wrapped in a wet sheet.

Daddy took off to town after the doctor. Mama laid a wet towel across Uncle John Ray's forehead and started sponging him down with a rag. He stopped muttering and got still, but the twitch stayed in his fingers: I fanned him with one of the cardboard fans the funeral home had put out for Granny's service, and tried to hold his hand, but his skin was red and dry and hellfire hot, and he shook too bad for me to keep a grip. His hands were huge, compared to mine.

We fanned and sponged. Uncle John Ray shook harder, his eyelids spasming open to show white, and Mama started to cry.

She changed the towel across his forehead and he growled in his throat, then whined. It was a high hoarse sound, and while Mama tapped his face and made shushing noises, his shadow started drifting out.

I dropped my fan and watched. It was darker than Granny's had been, the tiny black motes more tightly packed. It moved slower too, out a little and back in. Fighting. Hesitating.

John Ray's whine cut off all at once, and in the silence his shadow swept out of him. It broke free in a rush and hurried upward, hovered at the ceiling, vanished.

He wasn't breathing anymore. I clenched my jaw and curled my fingers into fists. This time Mama was the one who screamed, but I knew she hadn't seen that one either.

***

There were no deaths for a while after that. I went to school and played baseball and played with Rufus, our old red coonhound, and almost forgot about seeing shadows.

The weekend after I turned ten, Rufus was hit by a county truck. The driver never stopped. I crawled into the ditch where Rufus had landed and wrapped my arms around his bloody head and begged him not to die.

He'd never been good at listening.

For a long time I sat down there holding his head, waiting to see the shadow crawl out of him and fly away.

It never happened. I didn't know why not.

***

My friends and I made our baseball field from a narrow empty lot next door to the Baptist church. The preacher was a tall big-boned man everybody called Brother Paul, and sometimes on Sunday afternoons after church he'd come out to the edge of our lot and watch our games, with his tie loose around his neck and his suit coat slung over his arm.

Seeing him out there one Sunday after Rufus died got me thinking about the shadows. When our game was over, I walked up to him and said I needed to ask a question.

His eyebrows went up—my people were Presbyterian when we bothered to be—but he let me come sit in the church to talk. It was a cool dark place, and rainbows striped the floor from the little colored glass windows.

Brother Paul listened while I told him about what I'd seen from Granny and Uncle John Ray. I was sure he'd bring up hell—Daddy always said Baptists were awful keen on hell—but he just made this low rumbling noise in his throat, like he was thinking about it and working up his mouth. Daddy always said Baptists liked to talk, too.

"Well, Jimmy Earl," he said after some quiet, "I can't rightly claim to have answers to all of God's mysteries, but it may just be you saw their souls going up to heaven. The Good Book says we flee like shadows. They were in a hurry to get home."

"What about Rufus?" I asked.

Brother Paul went quiet, then rumbled again. His shoulders worked under his shirt. Finally he said, "Well...there's no need for dogs to have souls, Jimmy Earl." He chewed his lip. "They can't sin. They don't have to be saved."

That wasn't an answer. I got up and walked home.

***

But I thought about souls a lot after that, especially the ones I didn't see.

Like Daddy. The year I turned fourteen, the cotton failed. He plowed it under and went to work at the cannery out from the other side of town, catching a ride back and forth every day with a member of the Baptist church who worked the same shift. When a massive heart attack dropped Daddy in his tracks mid-shift one day, I was in third period English. I didn't get to see his soul-shadow leave, didn't get to see if it rushed up or sank down.

I didn't know if they ever went down, toward hell. For Mama's sake I tried not to think about that.

Mama sold the plot we'd grown cotton on and went to work at the cannery. I started working after school and on weekends for Seth Carver, who grew wheat instead of cotton; he gave me odd jobs while I waited to get old enough to drive a grain truck, and I tried not to get caught staring at his daughter.

She almost made me forget about seeing shadows, too.

***

I was sixteen when the accident happened.

Seth and two of his farmhands were in a silo walking down the wheat when they broke through the crusted top layer and sank into the settled grain underneath. Six hours later when the rest of us got them out, they were blue-faced and limp, with wheat kernels packed in their mouths.

For weeks afterward I could barely sleep. I kept imagining sinking into loose wheat like quicksand. I wondered if they'd screamed, or if they'd prayed. I wondered if their shadows had been able to get free, and if they'd risen to the ceiling of the silo, or if the soul dust had been lost, scattered in the wheat.

***

The first two times I asked Seth Carver's daughter Audrine out on a date, she said no. The third time I asked, she said, "Well, if it'll keep you from looking so pitiful, I'll go."

Six months after our first date, when I asked her to marry me, she said yes. She didn't say whether I looked pitiful or not.

I was nineteen when we got married. Audrine was twenty. A year later, our Sally was born, and as I sat next to Audrine's hospital bed and held my daughter in my arms, searching her little scrunched face for some trace of myself and finding only my stick-straight eyebrows, I found myself thinking that this was it. No more death, no more shadows. Audrine's mother had held onto her land. I had a good job driving a grain truck. I had a wife, a daughter, a future.

I should have known it wouldn't last.

***

When Sally started to cough, we thought it was just a cold. She was eight months old; the weather had been damp.

When she started whooping, we knew we were wrong.

Audrine took her into town to the doctor. Sally got her nose swabbed and her finger pricked. She had a fever. She got medicine.

She didn't get better.

I'll never forget that Tuesday night. Audrine was cleaning up from supper and I was in our bedroom, standing over Sally's crib, watching her fitful sleep. Lord knew none of us had gotten much of that lately.

I tickled her chin. She hiccuped awake and started to cough and cough, and suddenly I was remembering Granny and her death rattle. Uncle John Ray's too-hot skin. Their souls coming out of their bodies in shadows and disappearing in front of my eyes.

Sally gasped in air with that horrible high sound, like Uncle John Ray had made. Her little lips were gray, drool slipping from her mouth. I tried to sit her up and thump her chest.

Then I saw her shadow.

It wasn't tattered like Granny's, or sleek dust like John Ray's. The darkness seeping out of Sally's mouth was almost solid, black as soot. It didn't stream off. It struggled, sliding back when she gasped again. It didn't want to leave.

I couldn't let it leave.

I laid her down and grabbed a pillow off the bed and put it over Sally's mouth. I pressed down. I had to keep her soul in.

"Sally?" Audrine walked into the room. "Jimmy E—*ohmygod!*"

Audrine shrieked and threw herself on me. "I'm trying to help!" I shouted, but she wouldn't let me shake her off. She clawed my face and snatched the pillow away, and I watched Sally's soul-shadow thrash out of her mouth and break away, up, up, faster than any I'd seen, and it was gone.

"I was trying to help," I said weakly. "I was holding it in. She could've lived if you'd let me hold it in."

Audrine slapped me and ran from the room. When the sheriff arrived, I told him about my baby's soul. He just looked at me with pity in his eyes and reached to handcuff me.

"I was trying to help," I said. "I was trying to help."

***

I got sent to a psychiatric hospital. Audrine got a divorce.

It's not too bad here. They listen to me when I want to talk about the shadows. About how I was trying to save my baby girl. I do what I'm told. I don't bother anybody. I take the pills. I get to use a spoon that's metal and not plastic.

Anything can hold an edge.

I made up my mind when Mama visited and told me Audrine had remarried. I don't know what I'll do yet. Maybe my throat. Probably my throat. I think that would take a long time.

Maybe I'll get to see it. I want to see it, the shadow coming out of me, see how thick my soul dust is. See where it goes and if Brother Paul was right.

I want to see my baby girl again.

I want to see if everybody really hurried to get home.

INHALE, EXHALE

SOMEHOW, OVER THE wind's howl, you hear yourself breathing.

Your shoulders ache dimly from the strain of your arms pulled behind your back and bound to your stake, but you lost feeling in your hands an hour ago. Your legs are numb up to your knees. The pain in your face has become a mask you wear, dull and stiff; your head is fixed in place, held by your hair, by the braid nailed into the wood.

You'd cried when you were lashed here in the twilight, when everyone hurried away, when your mother stroked your hair but wouldn't look you in the eyes. You stopped crying when you realized the sting down your cheeks was the wind-torn tracks of your tears, freezing to your skin.

There was no fanfare. There never is. Now all you do is blink, and breathe, and wait.

When the first breath of winter skirts across the land, someone has to be sacrificed. It's the way. Flesh and blood must be traded for a few more weeks of strong sun and clear skies, for a safe end to the late harvest, for a peaceable season bereft of storms. When the gift isn't given, the crops shatter on the vine, the cattle freeze beneath mounds of snow. It's always been the way.

You cried at the thought that anyone else could have been chosen. You stopped when you realized there was no reason it shouldn't be you.

Nothing moves when you try to flex your rope-bound limbs. You drag in a deep breath, and something breaks within your nostrils, spilling down your face. You feel nothing, taste nothing; only the slowness of the ooze tells you it's blood. You open your mouth to breathe out, but there's merely a muted tingle when your wetted lips rip apart from one another.

Whatever plume your exhalation makes, it's swallowed by darkness. The gale shifts, tearing at the tatters it's made of your clothes, curling around and into you like a living thing with breath of its own. The knifing pain the frigid air made in your chest at sunset is now only a distant twinge.

You blink. You breathe. It's becoming difficult. You have the slow, cold-glazed thought that you'll be buried at sunrise, and you're surprised to find you still have a few tears left.

It had to be you. It always had to be you.

You breathe in.

You breathe out.

You wait.

THE TOMB WIFE

REMIÈRE IS DEAD.

The boy who had come to the mouth of the catacombs would have fled at the sight of my face, had he not been tasked with his message. Now I prowl the foggy churchyard of Saint Vincent of the Shroud, waiting for the one who will come to fetch me, gathering dew on my feet. My dress is grey velvet—a mourning shade, and one unsoiled by the grave—but living among the dead, I had forgotten shoes. Remière would have laughed at that, as he laughed at so many other things.

Now there isn't anyone here to laugh. I walk among the graves and mouth the names on the stones, mouth the words that come to me, work life back into my rusty voice. I speak my name, *Delphine, Delphine,* but get no answer.

I'm a ghoul, after all. No one comes to speak with me.

***

There is a stranger at the grave of Marie-France Remière, a resting place I know not only for its occupant but also for the statue that stands guard over it, a weeping Madonna that had once adorned Remière's back garden: Our Lady of Sorrows.

Madame Remière had been delicious.

He, this stranger, has brought nothing to her grave but

himself; no flowers, no trinkets. He wears a brown tweed suit and a long black coat against the damp, and his hat shadows much of his face, but when the limp wet leaves squelch under my feet, he turns to me a smile half-hidden under his bushy white moustache, and says, "Delphine."

I stop in place. Is he the one sent to wait for me? "You know me."

"Remière spoke of you often." He doesn't notice the grating squeak of my voice, or he pretends for politeness. "He was young when you met, yes? Just starting as the town butcher, making ends meet by robbing graves for a doctor's studies." He steps away from the grave and toward me, hand extended. "I'm Auguste Cardin. I was the doctor."

I've never heard this name; Remière never spoke it. To him there was always just "the doctor." I stare at his hand, the smooth palm and neat, short nails, for a full three seconds before I remember to touch it with my own. He smells of cologne and carbolic soap, and the pink of life is in his cheeks. My own fingernails are long and cracked, with burial earth beneath them. "Why are you here?"

Dr Cardin releases my hand. "Remière has left you a gift. It was his dying wish that I find you." He touches my uncovered hair and takes my chin in his hand, staring at my face. "He was right. You're beautiful."

I am thin, barefoot, ashen-skinned and yellow-eyed. I am not beautiful. I say nothing.

✳✳✳

Twenty years have passed since I last saw Remière, and since I last dared creep from the burying grounds to his back garden, when the Madonna still stood sentinel there. This man Cardin could buy his transport to any destination in this city, but no driver in France would take a fare from my hand. We walk.

I fidget on Cardin's arm. The sun hasn't yet broken the fog, and the cobblestone streets are smudges of soft tan and grey.

"When did Remière...die?" I'm an eater of the dead, yet the word sticks in my throat. Remière of the broad shoulders and big, brash laugh and curiously gentle hands, now still and empty and cold as clay. I can't picture it. "Tell me."

Cardin makes a rumbling thoughtful noise. "Six hours ago. The city clock had just rung two bells. His heart had been failing for some time, and I'd been treating him with morphia." He catches my hand awkwardly and squeezes. "It was quite painless, Delphine, I promise you."

That's no comfort to me. "I don't understand," I murmur at last. "I thought I was only a curiosity to him. A novelty."

"You were more than that to Claude Remière." Cardin sighs. "Much more."

"I'm not even human," I protest. The streets are empty, yet I feel watched from every angle. "What could he possibly have given me?"

"What he felt you most deserved." The doctor shifts his grip to my elbow, and guides me down the Rue Montaigne. Remière's house is at the end, blue slate and polished glass. "His heart."

✱✱✱

The thin young woman who meets us at the door, garbed head to toe in black, has Remière's black hair and his high forehead, but her eyes are pale and cold instead of brown and sparkling, and her mouth is a tight downward line. I know she's Remière's daughter, named Marie, and she doesn't offer her hand. "Dr Cardin. I see you've brought the beast."

I flinch from Cardin, and Marie's lips twist up mockingly. I stare into her eyes, seeing myself, seeing my pointed teeth and the forward thrust of my jaw, and I want to hate this girl; I want to say, *your mother died bearing you, and before you there were five stillborn sons, each wrapped by his midwife in a bloody sheet and buried in the garden beneath that statue of the Virgin; but it wasn't Our Lady of Sorrows who bore the meat away, and your father called it the best end he could have wanted for them.*

I find my voice. "Marie. My name is Delphine."

She steps back from me, wide-eyed. "Jesu, it speaks! Cardin, what have you brought into my house?"

"I'm just following your father's wishes, Marie," he answers. "You know the terms."

"Yes. I know." Marie spits at me and wipes her mouth. "My mother suffered and died to give my father even one child, and he loved a monster. A *monster*." She shakes her forefinger, its nail red-lacquered, in my face. "And my father died still so besotted with you that I can't even inherit properly until you've eaten his heart!"

His heart. So that's what Cardin had meant. I turn away from her, stumbling. "I shouldn't be here—"

"Delphine." Cardin takes me by the shoulders and shakes me, but gently. "No. You must. You must. It's what he wanted." He puts his face close to mine and whispers, "Even if it benefits Marie."

"She takes what she came for." Even without seeing her face, I can hear Marie's teeth scrape together. "Just that, and not a fiber more. I hold you responsible, Cardin."

"Of course you do." He puts an arm around my shoulders and guides me past her, toward a staircase. "Come, Delphine. Remière is waiting."

***

Remière's house is neither large nor particularly imposing; the walls are dark, the carpet stained, the furniture worn in a way that suggests comfort. The gas lamps glow inside globes of amber glass and cast flickering shadows. I spot a shawl thrown over a chair, and a bouquet of dried flowers lies in the fireplace atop a mound of ashes, but I see nothing I can call decoration. He was a butcher, after all, and a widower, and would have been practical.

I wonder if it looked different when his wife was alive.

"You must forgive Marie," Cardin tells me at the top of the stairs. "She's young. She's only just found out."

I stare down the narrow hallway. "But I *am* a monster."

He leads me to the room at the end of the hall and opens the door. I stand in the doorway while Cardin lights the lamps. This is Remière's bedroom, as plain as the rest of the house; the bed is large and roughly fashioned, and I deliberately keep my gaze down, away from the large familiar shape beneath the pulled-up sheet. A red-upholstered chair is drawn up to the bedside, the only bright color I've seen, and a black leather bag sits on its seat. Cardin takes up the bag and occupies the chair. "My surgical tools," he says apologetically. "Marie must have a glimpse before I make the repairs."

I skirt the bed carefully. The faintest odor of beginning decay rises to meet me, making my palate tingle and my stomach knot. I haven't eaten in days. "If I eat him when he's buried," I say slowly, "will she know?"

I look up, but Cardin's attention is on a threadbare patch in the rug. "He'll be cremated tomorrow." He meets my gaze and gives me the barest of smiles. "Remière never expressed his wishes for the rest of his body."

Just his heart. I study Remière's form beneath its covering, and draw back the sheet. The whisper of death, of *food*, intensifies, and my mouth waters.

He had startled me, that first night, breaking into the crypt in which I was feeding. He'd startled me the next night by coming back to look for me, and the next, until I'd realized that I was his focus, and his tomb-defiling work had become an afterthought. Remière had been a skilled butcher even then, fifty years ago, carving the choicest meat for me from his prizes when he'd been no older than Marie.

I should tell her we made love for the first time in an empty grave.

Remière's curly hair is silver now instead of black, and his beard is almost white, and the lines on his face are deep; but his brows have kept their color, and his shoulders have kept their breadth. I climb onto the bed, pulling my skirts up over my thighs as I settle myself on his hips and rest my hands on his shoulders.

Even his death pallor makes my skin look grey. I kiss his forehead, his eyebrows, his mouth, and I realize I haven't forgotten how to weep.

"Do you know"—Cardin's voice jerks me upright—"he had names for you. His tomb wife, his corpse bride, Delphine des Goules." He's twirling a scalpel in his fingers, studying the gleam of the lamplight on the blade. "Shall I help you?"

"No," I say, and I open Remière's skin with my nails.

I shove my fingers through the flesh between his fourth and fifth ribs, a skill I'd learned young, and pry them apart, the bones cracking as they loosen. I worm my hand into the gap and curl my fingers around Remière's heart, still faintly warm, and pull it free, holding it in my hands, taking in the maze of arteries and the padding of visceral fat.

Then I honor his wish, and my hunger.

***

"He should have been yours." That's all Cardin says, afterward, as he wipes my mouth and my hands, as he twists Remière's wedding ring from his finger and presses it into my palm. I hide it in my bodice and keep silent. He leads me back down the stairs as I suck away the blood still edging my nails. "Delphine, if you need anything—"

"No." I want no more promises to devour; I've had enough. "Thank you. No. Let me go."

Marie is sunk into a chair beside the cold fireplace. She springs up as Cardin leads me to the door. "I suppose it's done?"

"It's done," Cardin answers. "I'll show you."

"Fair enough." The girl glides up to me with her hands on her hips, looking me over. Abruptly she grabs my hair and wrenches my head back, and sweetly says into my ear, "If I see you again, beast, I'll have you hunted down and burned."

"Marie!" Cardin shouts. She lets me go; I snarl at her; Cardin comes between us and backs me out into the street.

"No, Delphine." We stand on the pavement and he rubs the back of my neck. "No. Go back to where you belong. Remember Remière. Forget his daughter."

He makes it sound simple, but I know it's not. "You asked me to forgive her."

"Yes. Will you try?"

"I'll try," I answer, "but someday she'll die, and I'm patient." Forgiveness, like love, is almost nothing to me. I still have Remière's flavor on my tongue and behind my teeth, salty and beefy and copper-sweet; I draw his ring from my bodice and slip it over my right thumb, bending my hand into a fist. I look up at Cardin and for the first time in two decades, I feel myself smiling. "Perhaps she'll even taste like her father."

A KISS OF FLESH

(for Lester Smith)

THE COLD IRON handle of the mausoleum's door shifts at my touch, unlocked, and I pause. Doubt gnaws at my gut as the package inside my coat shifts, and for the thousandth time I wonder what I'm doing. My hands bear fresh calluses and blisters from the spade, garden soil clinging to the whorls of my skin.

My fingers cramp as I open the door. A sprinkle of rust flakes showers down on me, but the squeak of the hinges is a whisper. Inside, all of the unused niches in the marble are filled with her little flickering lamps, their smoke twining up through the gratework in the ceiling. Inside, on the solitary slab, she sits cross-legged in a ragged white dress; her bare feet are long, graceful, the nails painted with a dark gloss. Her hands lie in her lap, the nails trimmed short and caked with dirt.

Her eyes are closed, her breathing even. *Waiting for me*, I think at first, before I realize: *asleep*.

A leaf, brown and crumbling, rests in the black mass of her hair. I pluck it out. She opens her eyes.

"Claude." Her voice is dry reeds and disuse, but she smiles.

"Delphine." A grin comes to my own lips before I remember the bundle in my coat, wrapped in oilcloth so it won't leak. Ghoul, monster, woman: she's more beautiful than the last time I saw her;

more beautiful than the first time, when my spade broke the surface of a grave and she looked up at me with a rib in her jaws. Infinitely moreso than the woman I'm forced to call my wife. "I brought you something."

Delphine slides to her feet, fits herself into my arms like a missing piece of me, kisses me with the sweet foulness of her mouth. When she pulls back, the light glistens on the long sharp facets of her canines. "Show me."

The oilcloth crinkles as I retrieve it, as I put it in her hands to open, to release the perfume of decay. She studies the small contents, the plump but blackening flesh; she spreads the tiny limbs wide, and her mouth creases in uncertainty. "You would bring this to me?"

I swallow, dry-mouthed. Never before has she refused one of my putrefying gifts, although never before has one been quite so personal. Still, I hope, I've known her too long, too well, for her to hate me. "Yes."

"Claude." She lifts her yellow eyes from the lifeless babe to my face, questioning. "This is *your* son?"

"He lived an hour, Delphine. It's been five days." When had her voice dropped to a whisper? When had mine? I cup her cheek in my hand, smearing earth across her skin. "I can't give him a better resting place."

"You honor me too much," she murmurs, and her grip on my dead child's body has become tender, maternal. She should have been a mother; she should have been a mother to this boy. He would have lived. "Will you stay?"

Tomorrow, in my garden, I'll rebury a little bundle of bones. Tonight, my place is here. "Yes."

Delphine cradles the infant to her breast with one hand, wraps the fingers of the other around my wrist. She digs in. "And when there are other sons?"

I lean in first, so that our foreheads touch; then I pull away to look her in the eyes. I'm going to Hell for this, but she's worth every step. "Then perhaps there will be other gifts."

She doesn't quite smile, but her eyes soften with the line of her mouth. She lets me go. "Shut the door."

I hear it while I'm turned away, the tearing-silk sound of her teeth sliding into flesh, and I smile.

INCISION

BREATHE. THAT'S IT. Just breathe. You're safe. I've got you.

Don't worry. You won't feel any pain. I can promise you that. And of course you can't move. Chemical paralysis. Very simple. Safer for us both. You're only...awake.

I want you awake.

I want you to see the work.

So beautiful, humans. Such specimens we make for each other, flesh caged in bone, vitality trapped in blood—

Who'd have thought the old man to have had so much blood in him?

There is so much blood in you.

I've kept most of it in.

I wish you could feel my hands. Feel *with* my hands: grasp your grey-pink lungs, watch them swell and shrink, wrap fingers around your heart and hold tight as it tries to jump free. I'm almost tempted to squeeze.

But I digress. I said I wanted you to see. Show you how perfect you are inside. How perfect I knew you would be.

I do have a mirror. Let me just lift your head—there.

Aren't you *marvelous*?

CLARY RECOLLECTED

I.
THE COLD, THE STILL

THIS IS CLARY: eight, blonde, blue-eyed, hypothermic.

The only thing Daddy had said to her was, "Maybe you can tell your bitch mother to think twice about cheating on me," and then he'd shut the door, and the light had gone out.

Clary doesn't know how long ago that's been.

She squirms and whimpers. She'd screamed and wet herself when he'd trifolded her into the chest freezer, urine soaking the stiffening legs of the pink Hello Kitty shorts she'd worn to Vacation Bible School this morning and pooling on the bags of frozen blueberries that roll like marbles under her hip. The air is frigid and stale, stinking of her pee, making her chest ache. Her pillow is the rock-hard turkey Mommy had bought last year for Thanksgiving and forgotten about.

Forgotten about.

Mommy won't know she's here.

Mommy won't know where to look for her.

Clary squirms again, tries to turn onto her back, but Daddy wrapped her up too tight: arms behind her back, duct tape around her wrists and elbows. Pee-streaked duct tape down her legs at thighs and knees and ankles, more duct tape pulling at her hair, holding the spit-soaked wad of a dirty gym sock in her mouth.

Her bare legs are burning with the cold, her toes numb. She scrabbles at the thick ice crust; her fingertips tear, and bleed, and stick. She tries to move her legs and scrapes her knees on the built-up frost. They leak.

"Mommy," she whines into the sock, tasting grime and wet cotton on her tongue, and starts to sob. The tears slide over her face, burning her eyes, rolling down the cheek that's pressed against the turkey. They make her skin stick to that too, but she can't feel it anymore. Snot congeals on the duct tape across her lips. Her eyelashes harden and break.

She breathes faster, the cold a saw-toothed knife in her narrow chest, and can almost see the puffs. Her fingertips throb, but she can't pull them free without ripping them further. Her watch chimes on her taped-up wrist: three beeps in the arctic darkness.

Clary tries to curl up tighter. Three beeps. Three o'clock. Mommy will be home at five.

Maybe that will be soon enough.

***

It was, somehow, but I miss my toes.

The hospital weeks are a blur. Somewhere in there, Mommy left Daddy. They got a divorce. I had to learn to walk again. All I really remember now is that I punched the inside of the freezer once, broke three of my fingers on the ice crust, and when my blood escaped, it smoked like boiling water.

By then my feet were blue.

I punched the bathroom mirror last night, and the gashes in my knuckles still smoked. It was the glass that bled.

If I pushed through? Pushed through the ice, the mirror, would everything right itself? Would the ice and glass give off vapor, and my flesh drip red? Would my blood boil off into the void? Was I hallucinating last night? Was I imagining the smoke?

This shit is what keeps me up at night, Alison.

I'm sorry. I'm sorry. I know you have to get up for work soon. I'll shut up and go to sleep. It just still gets to me sometimes, you know? I can still taste that damned sock. I want to be normal, I just, I just want to be *normal.*

I know, I'm sorry, don't—

II.
A DRY LAND AND A WILDERNESS
*(Jackson-Madison County General Hospital,
15 March 2012, 4:02AM)*

John Frank has been set as a seal and a warning: for being in the wrong place, for not looking back.

His life is braided up in tubes and bags (tracheostomy with ventilation, 18-gauge peripheral cannula, normal saline, AB negative) and blood-black remnants that spear his gums with the monofilament used to stitch his lips together, to hide the shards of broken glass and shredded tongue. The line was twelve-pound test; the needle an upholstery one, beaten into a curve.

Meanwhile, Alison (twenty, brunette, 2010 softball MVP) sits on her steps in the Campbell Street projects, counting the cash in John Frank's wallet—

twenty-nine dollars, thirty-one cents, unwrapped condom, expired driver's license, two one-cent stamps. Who keeps one-cent stamps?

—because he's passed by her checkout lane and grabbed her ass for the last goddamn time.

The Louisville Slugger between her knees cries out for John Frank with a rust-dark voice: her girlfriend Clary had left a brighter streak, because Clary kept her up last night, wouldn't shut up with that shit about her old man and the freezer, the punching and the ice and the blood. Clary had even taken the last Vicodin.

She's cooling, now, in their bedroom, blonde hair matted black to the pillow, pieces of teeth scattered across the floor. At least her neck is a good clean break.

Alison's abscessed jaw throbs, sending black spots and red veining lines up into her vision. She maybe hadn't meant to hit Clary so hard, but done is done. Really, Clary deserved that. It was the last Vicodin, and no more till Friday. Fuck Clary.

The paramedics skidded in for John Frank fifteen minutes ago: three minutes more, and they'd have been too late. The police have just arrived. Alison slings the bat over her shoulder and walks out to meet them, passing the guy from down on the corner, the one who shines shoes and talks to himself, who grazes her with eye contact and flinches away to walk wide of the noise.

For John Frank—pillar of salt, machine-breathing—his upper left molars, jammed into his maxillary sinus, work out their salvation in blood clots and pus.

For John Frank, scheduled to flatline at five forty-five

(**thromboembolism**, *noun*, formation in a blood vessel of a clot that breaks loose and is carried by the bloodstream to plug another vessel)

the only kindness granted is a bone left unbroken, the intermediate phalanx of his right ring finger: his signet ring, a gift from his grandfather, will be found by one of the cops in Alison's back pocket.

Alison will die in three months' time, in the yard at Southwest Correctional, on the wrong end of a plastic knife.

But for now, let her have this victory.

III.
ESCAPE ROUTES AND RECIPE PLANNING

You're safe, Clary. I've got you. I don't know how anyone overlooked you.

It's a shame I didn't get to you sooner, but when Alison was taken away, I didn't immediately think you might be inside. I might have found you still alive, and that would have been better.

You could have watched.

I'm sorry about your face. You always were the prettier one.

At least this way you won't feel any pain.

But I wish you were awake. I want you to see the work.

So beautiful, people. Wrapped in skin, caged in bone, trapped in blood. Who'd have thought the old man to have had so much blood in him? Somebody famous wrote that once.

There's so much blood in you.

You were prettier before I cut your throat, but the blood had to come out. It still steamed, a little.

I wish you could feel my hands. Feel me wrap fingers around your heart and squeeze, squeeze, until your throat stops leaking.

How I wish you could see this. How I wish I could show you how perfect you are inside, how perfect I knew you would be.

Let me lift your head and open your throat.

Smile for the camera, Clary.

***

Somewhere, on a side road between Brownsville and Memphis, I threw your head off a bridge. No identification. No dental. It's for the best.

I'm sorry, Clary. It really wasn't supposed to be you. I wanted Alison to pay for what she did to John Frank. He was an all right guy, John. Tipped well when I shined his shoes. Too good to deserve to die like that. Just like you, too pretty to go around wearing a black eye from another woman's hand.

I almost didn't look for you. Almost stopped myself. I did this once before; that's why I'm not a butcher now, why I've shined shoes since I got out of that special hospital. I don't want to go back there. Everything was white and the walls were all wrong.

But I couldn't let you go once I found you in that apartment.

You're holding up well, what I could keep of you, what would fit in the Ziplocs in my cooler. Shoulder roast. Flank steak. Short ribs. I can boil your neck for broth and scraps, with your hands and feet. Little bones, little slivers of meat, the kind of leftovers a good dog can dispose of. Carrots, onions, celery at any Walmart: soup of you, for me.

A ball of fat, though you never had much to spare. A scrape of marrow, because I cracked your thighbones. The muscle there's long and lean. I'll have to slow cook you then, girl. Sweet onions, fingerling potatoes, a little honey glaze on the carrots.

Remind me to get more ice when we get to Senatobia. I can't have you going off on me now.

I don't know where we're going. Farther south than Tennessee. Maybe a little place out in the woods along the river bottom, some empty shell of a house with a gravel road and no electricity, with a creek or a well. A good cook can do a lot with just a fire and a pit. I want to hide us somewhere and leave this truck behind.

I wonder if anybody else has found what I left of you yet. I wonder if anybody's thought to look for me. The crazy butcher, the shoeshine man, still touched in the head. I wonder if anyone's screaming over you.

I've got a cousin in Holly Springs, if you can hold out that long. Old, blind, wouldn't know good beef from bad; I could put dog meat on the grill and he'd think it was prime rib. Lives on the edge of a national forest. Might just be the escape we're after, one way or another.

I'll take good care of you, girl.

I know you wonder why I'm doing this, a strange thing for a dead stranger. We lived in the same project and you wouldn't know my name if I told it. You never had shoes worth shining, but you walked past my corner every morning and you smiled at me. Slipped me a dollar or two when that girl wasn't looking. Never called me crazy like everybody else. You deserve to be remembered for that.

This is what I can do. This is the memorial I can give you.

It's time to stop for that ice. Don't go anywhere.

Be a good girl, Clary.

RADIANCE

THE THUMP HAD come from the basement, and so does the heat. You're sweltering by the time you reach the bottom of the steps, but the vents are all cold except the one in the far corner, the one by the body. It's the third one this month.

You look up first, to the beam overhead and the snapped cord, then down to bent ligatured neck and shock-splayed limbs. A tiny gash along the jawline draws your attention, making your face sting with recognition. You kneel and grasp the chin—sweat-slick, too warm, slipping in your fingers and making your skin crawl— and turn the head, looking into your own glazed eyes. The corner vent has begun to glow dull red, and the hair, *your* hair, is starting to singe.

Maybe you should let it. Three times this month, and you keep *finding* yourself like this. Maybe you should let it burn; maybe that will give you answers. You unbutton your damp collar and run a hand over your razor-nicked face, breathing the acrid stench of crisping hair, and watch your corpse's fingers twitch and curl.

SAY (PART I)

SAY SOMETHING.

Say I'm dreaming. Say I'm hallucinating. Say this isn't really happening.

Say it's not really you splayed here on the kitchen floor, limbs curled loose like a broken spider's, your hair powdered white from its pillow of flour spilling from the bag tipped half off the counter. You always make a mess in here, always such a goddamn mess. What were you thinking? Say it. Say what you were thinking.

Say the drop of blood on the linoleum didn't leak from the crook of your elbow. Say the tourniquet's not still on your arm, the needle's not still in the vein. Say your skin isn't ashen and your lips aren't gaping blue beneath the foam. Say your eyes aren't open, aren't fixed, aren't glazed.

Say you'll wake up if I jostle your shoulder or tug my fingers through your hair just so, like always. Say you'll wake up, or I will. Say it's just another of my nightmares and you're fine. We're both fine. Warm. Pink. Breathing.

Say you're breathing. Please say you're breathing. Say the pulse I feel when I press my fingertips to your carotid isn't just my own. Say, as I kiss your cheek and stroke your hair back and snag a few strands on your earring, that it's me who's feverish and not you who's cold.

Say I don't have to do what I know comes next. 911. Ambulance. Sirens. You, carried away. Me, left behind. Say my last sight of you won't be with a shroud over your face.

Say it was a mistake. Say it was an accident. Say you didn't choose this.

Say it wasn't supposed to be like this. Say it's nothing I did. Say it's not my fault. Say that loudest of all.

But say something, damn you.

Say something.

Anything.

THE SEPULCHRE BRIDE

LATUA KISSED WITH an unclean mouth.

I was four when my mother died, trying to bear me a brother who only followed her into the grave. I was eight when Papa married Latua, old enough to notice that the village women stifled whispers behind their hands when we passed by, but still too young to quite understand the significance they attached to a short courtship. Papa had gone to visit Mama's grave and met Latua in the churchyard.

What she was doing there, if she'd lost a sweetheart of her own, I never knew. I only knew that Papa married her six weeks later in the registrar's office and that was the first day I saw her, with a veil over her face: mousy, yellow-eyed, wax pale, with a pinched set to her mouth as though her teeth ached. Her French was perfect but her accent odd, and she spoke her vows as though the words were a mystery.

To me she was nothing like beautiful.

I asked Papa, later, why he'd chosen her; why I hadn't met her sooner; why they'd been wed by the registrar and not a proper clergyman. He only patted my head. "I'm a lonely man, Stéphanie, and Latua's kind to me."

It was the only answer he ever gave.

***

Latua was not unkind to me. I could agree with Papa on that much: she was not unkind.

The first months of the marriage were awkward. The servants whispered, and Papa sent them away. Only the cook stayed, along with the tutors who came every weekday for my lessons. Latua picked at her food, excusing herself from every meal after only a few bites and causing Madame Ballou—the cook—to grumble incessantly about the waste.

"She eats like a bird," the old woman complained. I dried dishes; she would accept no help from Latua, who at any rate seemed utterly lost in the kitchen. "Less than a bird."

"I think her teeth hurt," I said.

Madame Ballou scowled at me. "I think your father has made a mistake. One he will pay for."

***

She wasn't the only one to think that way.

Mama had been a churchgoing woman and Papa, for her sake, had humored her. But when we all attended Mass the Sunday after Papa married Latua, we walked into Saint Vincent of the Shroud and were met with stares, whispers, craned necks.

Latua kept her head down and her hands in her lap. I leaned against her, embarrassed but mostly bored; the church was dark and stifling, and I had no real idea of why so many people stared at us. Then Father Didier stopped in the middle of his homily on the Good Samaritan, stared my father in the face, and said abruptly: "We must recognize the demonic when it is in our midst."

Latua twitched and knotted her fingers together. "What does *that* mean?" I whispered, but Papa only waved me off. He was red-faced and scowling.

We didn't go back.

At home, things seemed little better. My mother's portrait hung in the dining hall, her painted silk dress a bright blue specter against a stormy background. Papa had thought it would keep me from forgetting, when I scarcely remembered anything to begin with—I had only scraps of memories, a song, a laugh, a warm smile. The woman in the portrait, with her dark eyes and rosy cheeks and tumbling blonde curls, may as well have been a stranger to me. For Latua, who was not beautiful and did not sing and painted only inexpertly, she must have been a weight to labor under; and I understood, I thought, why my father's odd new wife never sat through meals, never spoke unless she was addressed first, and roamed the upper hallways barefoot at odd hours of the night long past my bedtime. I could hear the whisper of her soles on the parquet floor.

My dog Beau Jacques hated her. He was small and shaggy and old, and when some sense of duty started bringing Latua to my bedroom every night to kiss my forehead, he never moved from his spot curled tight against my side, but he would lift his head and growl. I didn't understand why he growled anymore than I understood why her goodnight kisses made me uneasy. Maybe it was merely her strangeness, but sometimes I thought I caught a sourness on her breath, like faint rot or bloody meat. Sometimes her teeth seemed too long and too sharp.

I didn't mention my misgivings. Papa seemed to love her for her peculiarities, and he had asked me to be kind, so every night I shushed Beau Jacques loudly and accepted Latua's kiss.

The word *stepmother* never entered my mind.

***

The day things began to change, Papa and Latua had been married six months. I woke to a wet foulness in my bed and on my nightgown, and Beau Jacques lying in the crook of my arm, stiff and cold, still curled tight.

I must have screamed. I made some noise, because it was Latua who stumbled into my room, wild-eyed and disarrayed as if she hadn't slept all night. There was earth on her feet and beneath her nails. "Stéphanie, Stéphanie, whatever's the matter?"

"It's Beau Jacques." I reeled up out of bed, my wet garment clinging to my legs. He had emptied himself in death. "I think—I think he's—"

"Hush, hush." She had seen. Quickly she drew the blanket and counterpane off my bed, pulled the sheet loose at the corners, and made a small bundle of it around Beau Jacques, scooping him into her arms. "It's all right, Stéphanie. It's all right. Wash yourself and change and I'll bring fresh sheets. Your father will take care of Beau Jacques."

She walked out of the room, trailing crumbs of soil. It was the most she'd ever said to me.

Papa buried Beau Jacques in the back garden, beneath a crabapple tree that had never fruited. I watched from the window while Latua stroked my hair and held my shoulders, and though my throat ached I couldn't bring myself to cry. I was afraid that if I cried I'd start to scream.

Afterward, I toyed at the piano and tried to read for my lessons, but nothing could hold my attention for long. Latua set up a blank canvas and began to paint the crabapple tree; she had washed her feet, but the soil was still under her nails.

At dinner that night, I was the first one to leave the table.

Latua didn't come to kiss me goodnight.

✳✳✳

I couldn't say what woke me. Maybe it was hunger; maybe it was my imagination, telling me that Beau Jacques was still beside me, wagging his tail, licking my arm. Maybe it was simply the full moon, making my room bright, luring me from my bed to the window.

Latua was in the garden.

She wore one of Mama's old day dresses, one that had been taken in to fit her thinness; the fabric was ragged where it touched the ground. I couldn't see what she was doing, because only her narrow back faced me, but she squatted in the freshly spaded dirt and her shoulders worked.

Suddenly I was afraid.

I crept back into bed, pulling the covers up to my chin, then over it. The sound of the back door closing made me poke my head out again, and this time I heard Papa's voice coming up the stairs.

"Are you sure it will be enough?"

"Yes." Latua sounded immensely tired; her steps dragged. "It's enough. For now." Then she stopped, not far from my door. "I should look in on—"

"No," Papa said. "Let her sleep."

"Do you think she heard anything? She'll know, Paul. I shouldn't have done it. Not so soon."

"Stéphanie won't know." My skin crawled at the sound of my name. "She won't know, Latua, and you need your strength. Come now, bathe and come to bed." Papa sighed. "Even if she notices, I'll tell her it was an animal. A fox or a badger. She'll believe me."

My face burned. I knew I'd seen no animal.

***

The next day I sulked through my lessons until noon, when my tutor left and I went to the kitchen, hoping Madame Ballou would spare me a slice of cake and a cup of cold tea. But it was her market day, and instead I found Latua sitting on the bench by the stove, paring potatoes with her nails.

For a moment I just stood and stared. Her head was down in concentration, her mouse-brown hair hanging in her face and frizzing from the heat, but her movements were quick and deft. The parings that fell into the pail at her feet were paper-fine.

She looked up and saw me and froze, wary-eyed. I simply got a knife from the cutlery drawer and sat beside her, and began to peel potatoes.

"I'm sorry you have to look at my mother every day." Immediately I felt my face warm—I didn't know why *that* had come out of my mouth—but Latua just shook her head.

"Your mother was a lovely woman. Your father's right to want you to not forget."

He puts you in Mama's cut-down dresses, I thought; but a heaviness in her voice made me look her in the face. Something had dried at one corner of her lips, something dark and mixed with hair.

No, not hair. Fur.

"Latua." It was the first time I'd called her by name. "You have something—"

She realized herself then, swiped her tongue at the spot and scrubbed it with the back of her hand. The dark flaked away.

Are you sure it will be enough? I had heard Papa ask her. *Are you sure it will be enough?*

"You did something." The words squeaked out, quiet. "I think you did something to Beau Jacques."

Latua put her half-peeled potato into the bowl with the unpeeled ones and started to her feet. I dropped my knife and gathered up a handful of her skirt. "No. Stay. Tell me."

"Stéphanie." Latua put a hand to her mouth hurriedly, like a woman about to vomit. "Please. Let me go. I'm sorry. I'm sorry."

Are you sure it will be enough?

"You don't eat our food. You don't drink tea or wine. Your eyes are *yellow*." I didn't let go. "Latua, what are you?"

My hold on her skirts kept her from straightening up, so she sat back down with a noise of defeat. Our gazes met and she looked away, drew a deep breath and let it out.

"It's really better that you know," she began. "Despite what your priest may think, I'm no demon." Her voice steadied, as though not looking at me made talking easier. "Stéphanie, I'm a ghoul."

Ghoul? I frowned. I knew the word from my fairy-tale books—the ones with pictures, that Father Didier said were sinful—but those slavering dog-faced creatures made Latua look like a goddess. I knew, too, what the books said about them. Tomb dwellers, and worse. "You eat dead things."

Slowly, she picked up a potato and began to strip its skin. "Yes."

A question began to beat unpleasantly at the back of my mouth. "...People?"

Latua paused. "Sometimes." She finished her potato, took my chin in her hand, and turned me to face her, as if she knew what I wanted to ask. "Your mother is still in her resting place. Watching your father, knowing he had to be a good man to stay so devoted so long...I love him, Stéphanie. I couldn't have married him if I'd done *that*." She let me go. "I wanted to tell you right away, I thought you should know, but Paul thought you would be afraid of me." Her hands shook. "Are you afraid? Do I frighten you?"

I studied her, and realized I'd begun to get used to her face. "No."

Latua sighed as though a weight had dislodged and fallen away. "Thank you. I *am* sorry about Beau Jacques. I told your father I could wait—"

She jammed her hand against her mouth again. Her throat spasmed and she coughed, hunching over. I got to my feet: was it the heat? Did she need air? "Latua? Latua, are you all right? Are you ill?"

"No, no." She coughed again, half heaving, and was tensely still for a long, long time. Finally Latua relaxed, exhaled slowly, and sat up straight again, swallowing hard.

"I'm not ill, Stéphanie." Latua's mouth twitched, and for the first time, I saw her smile. She put a thin arm around me and pulled me closer. "I'm not ill. I'm pregnant."

✳✳✳

When Latua's time came, my father ushered one of the town midwives up the stairs, planted me firmly in a chair in the parlor, and told me not to move till I was called for.

I knew better than to protest. Latua wasn't Mama, but he was afraid all the same.

Hours passed.

I expected it to be noisier. I'd heard women gossiping in the market about how this girl or that had awakened neighbors or roused half the town with her labor screams, but Latua only moaned and panted and growled, and from my downstairs perch even those noises were faint. She didn't scream. I wondered if it was easier for ghouls.

What I didn't expect was the midwife throwing the door open and tromping down the stairs, her hand in a bloody bandage. "That ugly woman's little fiend has *teeth!*" she shrieked at me, and stalked out into the street, slamming the door.

The silence that followed was very loud and very long.

I sat with my hands on my knees and waited, ears still faintly ringing. Finally, Papa came to the top of the stairs. "Stéphanie?"

I turned to look up at him. "Is Latua all right?"

"Latua's fine." He was pale as a ghoul himself, but smiling. "She's fine. Come, come see your sister."

I went up after him. Madame Ballou was gathering the soiled sheets, and wagged a finger at me. "Mind the little one. She bit the midwife."

Latua, propped up on half a dozen pillows with a tiny bundle at her breast, only laughed tiredly. "That dreadful woman deserved it." She beckoned me close, and put the bundle in my arms. "Thankfully, she looks like your father."

I studied the tiny scrunched face. The baby had Papa's black hair, just like me, but she looked too red and squashed for me to see any real resemblance. She opened one eye, just for an instant, and I caught a glimpse of yellow.

I sat on the side of the bed and held my new sister close. "What's her name?"

"Delphine." Papa stroked Latua's hair with one hand, and mine with the other. "We've called her Delphine."

BABY

MARION'S FIRST IDEA that anything was wrong came at the tickle between her toes, just after she'd shut off the water.

She glanced down into the slowly draining soapy water and saw them: the whip-thin black tendrils, curling between and around her toes first, tugging as if curious, then thickening up through the drain and skating over the tops of her feet. She stood perfectly still for three seconds, until a spasm of anxiety made her shiver and drive her fingers into the mass of her wet blonde hair.

But the snaking dark lengths wrapped around her ankles and glided halfway up her calves, and Marion drooped in resignation, leaning forward till her forehead touched the clammy wet tile. Baby was hungry.

She didn't know what it was, actually—some species of leech, maybe, knotted up down below like a rat king—or how it had got into her shower drain, or even how far it reached in other directions. Maybe in different houses, different wriggling ropes latched onto different legs. Maybe—

The tendrils tightened their collective grasp. Marion tensed, anticipating pain, but as always none really came. Brief rasping stings lapped toward her knees like aggressive cats' tongues, but then she was numb, numb as a stone, too numb to be afraid.

Then the creature, feeding, began to sing.

It was nothing Marion heard with her ears. The low rough fluting began beneath her skin, wormed its way deeper like seeking fingers, like tentacles, sheathing the innermost spaces between her organs in wavering, haunting cacophony. The dappled walls of the shower fell away, and as the song crept higher through her throat and toward her brain, it seemed that Marion's skin and skull fell away too. Odd stars sparked and warped behind her eyelids and between her teeth as the song receded, became a pulse, as if the cosmos held and rocked her in some vast welcoming womb.

Baby, the creature said, though to which of them it referred, she couldn't be sure.

Time unwound. The pulse weakened and stilled; the tendrils receded. Marion's cosmic nest gradually faded to the gleaming damp walls of her shower, and she stayed still for a long time before she could brace herself to step out on the mat. She raked both hands through her tangled hair again and looked down.

The tapering welts that curved toward her kneecaps still oozed blood sluggishly. In a few minutes there would be scabs, and tomorrow the scabs would peel off to reveal vermilion stippling its way up her skin, and the next day the vermilion would be gone, until the next time.

Marion reached for a hand towel to blot the most egregious ooze. It had taken more than usual this time, would probably take more the next time and the next; but Baby was hungry and had to be fed, and those moments of comfort, of song and slow-turning galaxies, were worth a little blood.

She wrapped herself in a towel and stepped out into her bedroom, still trailing blood, still tasting stars.

GRAVECHILD

IT'S SNOWING AGAIN: a fine powder that fills the graveside urns and dusts the outstretched wings of the marble cherubs. This morning I pulled on two dresses and a pair of workman's boots, and it's not quite enough to block out the chill.

The catacombs beneath Saint Vincent of the Shroud are older than the church itself, older than the graves in the churchyard. The old padlocked chain at their entrance, beneath which I creep every day, has been lost to rust and replaced more times than I can count. But the catacombs are clean enough, warm and dry, full of empty spaces and, more importantly, full of bones. Old bones have helped ghouls weather many a long winter; my own earliest memory is of my mother spooning bone meal into my mouth.

But winter also brings death with the cold, and fresh graves, and meat. It's into one of these I've dug, scooping aside loose soil and prying open the plain wooden coffin, when I hear the carriage approach.

It stops at the churchyard gate. Another hearse, I think, another funeral, and I burrow deeper into the grave, ready to scrape the soil down and bury myself with my feast until the mourners have gone. But after a moment, a whip cracks and the horses' hooves clatter, moving away down the street. A visitor, then, come to pay his respects.

I hunker down and begin to rake the earth down from overhead. It's always the new graves that draw the most visitors. And yet, as seconds pass, I hear no footsteps and no voices. The living like to talk to their dead. Carefully, a little curious, I push the grave soil aside again and raise my head above its edge. There's only a woman standing close by the gate, wearing a long black coat and no hat. She turns in a slow half-circle, her back to me, as though she's searching for a grave she hopes to recognize.

Then she shouts.

"Monster! Where are you, monster? Come out, beast, I know you're here!" The voice is thin, cracked, but familiar.

It's Marie Remière.

Despite the knot tightening in my stomach, I lever myself out of the grave and hurriedly claw the dirt into place: the snow will hide it soon enough. I brush myself down, shake my skirts, seize a handful of snow-wet leaves and scrub the blackened blood from my mouth. I approach her from behind, slowly; she still hasn't seen me, hasn't even turned around.

"Marie?" My voice is strong from practice; she gives a little cry and whirls around, backing up against a stone. I hold out my open hands. "Marie. It's Delphine."

She stares at me and says nothing. Only two years have passed since I last saw this girl, yet she looks as though she's aged ten: her pale eyes are wild, her thin mouth sharply lined, and grey has begun threading through her curly black hair. Beneath her coat I can see her shoulders trembling like a frightened rabbit.

I try again. "Marie. You called for me. I'm here."

"You're *filthy*." She spits the word, and for just an instant she's the girl who'd seethed at my presence two years ago, who'd hated me because her father had loved me. But just as quickly, the bravado passes, and she puts her face in her hands. "Delphine. Oh, God, Delphine, I need your help."

✳✳✳

Just beyond the churchyard gate, only a short walk away, there lies a child's grave—long emptied—and beside it, an ornate iron bench. I take Marie's hands and lead her there, brush off the snow and make her sit. "I don't understand. How can you possibly need my help?"

Marie brushes a hand through her hair, dislodging snow. She makes eye contact in increments, glancing, looking away, her cheeks staining red.

"I have a daughter," she says at last. "I met a man, after my father died. Anton Gaultier—ah, you don't know the name. He's a painter, a painter of fancies. Blond, handsome, always smiling. He charmed me, and I..." There's shame in her voice as well as on her face, but a little note of pride, too. "I had Angèlie."

I study her hands: they're bandaged, and she wears no rings. "Did you marry this man?"

"No." Her mouth tightens miserably. "He promised me, of course. After I had the baby, after things settled down. But Angèlie was born and Anton never settled." She huffs, her breath pluming out white in the cold. "A week ago he moved out of the house. He took Angèlie." Marie's voice cracks. "He has a pair of rooms in the Rue Bernier. Number nine. I've gone there every day—I've come from there now. I've begged his landlord to let me in. I've begged Anton himself. I've begged for hours, I've offered money. Anything, to get my daughter back. She's only sixteen months old, she needs me!"

Her teeth chatter. She's shivering even as tears begin to creep down her cheeks. "I stood in the street this morning and beat at the door until my fists bled and all he did was laugh at me through the keyhole!"

Oh, this girl. "Marie, what can I do? You hate me."

"I *need* you!" she sobs, grabbing at my sleeves. "I have no one! I have no father, I have no family, I can't even go to the police. Anton is Angèlie's father, I can't just keep her from him."

"There's Dr Cardin—" I begin.

"The doctor died in London six months ago."

And he'd been so kind to me. I sit back against the cold damp metal. "...All right, Marie. Tell me how you think I can help you."

"You can get her back." She fumbles in her coat and draws out a folded scrap of newspaper. "It's an advertisement from this morning."

I scan the words. Number nine, Rue Bernier. Artist wanting models. Deformities, illnesses, and physical peculiarities preferred. Discretion promised.

I crumple the paper in my fist and push away, scowl at her. "*Deformities.* Physical *peculiarities.* You only came here because you think I'm some...some *grotesquerie.*"

"I'm sorry." It's a broken whisper; Marie's crimson-faced now. "Anton's always loved the unusual. The strange, the...yes, grotesque. I thought that you...that you might be striking enough to appeal to him." She reaches forward and seizes my hands. "Please, Delphine. Please. My father loved you. If that means anything at all to you, please help me get my daughter back."

Striking. *Striking,* because for once she can't bring herself to say *monstrous* or *ugly.* "All right. I'll try." I want to say no, but I know I can't. "I make no promises, Marie. But I'll try."

✱✱✱

The Remière family home in the Rue Montaigne is just as I'd seen it two years earlier: dark, worn, comfortable. Aside from the covered easel in one corner of the parlor, and the crib and tiny ruffled clothes in the bedroom, Marie has changed practically nothing. "You should bathe first," she says, brisk now that she's home, "and then I'll dress you."

Dress me. As if I'm not a monster now but a doll to suit her purposes. But I bathe myself in icy water in her clawfoot tub, scrubbing off the churchyard earth, and for a few minutes I let myself imagine what it would have been like to live in this house, to sit at Remière's table and sleep in his bed. I wonder if he ever imagined the same.

I towel myself off roughly. Right now that's not important.

***

Marie has one dress that fits me well enough: a soft red springtime piece with short sleeves and gauzy, layered skirts bearing a cherry-blossom pattern. The bodice laces up, and the décolletage is low enough to make me wonder how her father ever approved of it. "I look like a whore."

"You look like an artist's model." Marie is kneeling at my feet, buttoning the neat black boots I'd stepped into. She looks up at me, mouth puckering, and adds sourly, "Sometimes there's no difference." Finishing, she stands and plucks at my hair. "I'll leave that alone. He'll like the raggedness. I can loan you a shawl, but he bought my coat and he'd know it." Staring at me, narrowing her eyes and sucking her teeth, she decides, "No face powder. You already look like a corpse. But a bit of rouge, something on your lips, and then..."

She squares her shoulders. "You'll get my daughter."

***

"Stay there." Marie had loaded me into a hansom with that explicit instruction. "Do whatever Anton wants, just don't leave without Angèlie."

It's late afternoon when the driver lets me out where the Rue Bernier branches off the main street, and I walk the rest of the way. It's more an alley than a street, too narrow and steep for anything but foot traffic, and by the time I've crested two hills to get to the leaning hovel marked as number nine, my chest aches from the cold. I take the crumpled newspaper scrap from a fold of my borrowed shawl and smooth it out against the door, then knock.

There's no answer at first. I'm about to knock again when the door rattles and a low male voice drifts out from the vicinity of the keyhole: "Yes?"

I bend down. The sound of a little girl's laughter is sharp and distinct. "Monsieur Gaultier? I've come about your

123

advertisement."

"Are you grotesque?" It's eager, brusque. "I have no time to waste on the mundane."

I can't help wondering how he'd react if I told him what I am. "I'm perfectly hideous."

He huffs, but I hear a bolt drawn, then others. The man who opens the door is almost too tall to fit its frame, broad-shouldered and muscular, with messy blond hair that hangs in his eyes. I crane my neck, trying to look past him for a glimpse of Angèlie—I can hear her babbling—but he puts a hand around my neck.

"You are not hideous." Anton Gaultier doesn't squeeze, but he could; I can feel the tension in his fingers. "You're an underdressed woman with a poor complexion and unfortunate teeth."

Angèlie giggles. If I can get inside, perhaps I can snatch her and be gone. I look up at him, then over his shoulder—and then he jerks my chin up.

"Although." He says it slowly and his brows lower. "The eyes. The eyes are unique. Very well." He steps back. "Come."

I have to duck under his arm to pass. I'm in a tiny dim room with a smoke-smudged window, full of easels and flickering oil lamps, and I can see a doorway into another. Mixed scents assault my nostrils: linseed oil, turpentine, sour milk, badly burned fish.

Underneath it all, I smell blood.

The tallest easel is uncovered, bearing a canvas painted black with wide rough strokes. At its foot, Angèlie sits on the floor, slapping a piece of butcher's paper with a paint-stained hand and giggling at her own fingerprints. Her feet are bare and her dress stained, but she's plump enough and rosy-faced, with blonde hair darker than her father's. Her eyes are murky.

I squat beside her while Anton locks the door. "Hello, little one," I say, and whisper, "Angèlie, your Mama sent me."

"Ma!" Angèlie crows, and Anton Gaultier scowls.

"Leave her alone." He comes up and puts a hand under my left arm, yanking me upright before I can stand, pulling me toward a chair in the center of the room. "Sit there. Let me see if you're worth my time."

I sit. "Is she your daughter, Monsieur?"

"She is not your business." He draws up a stool and a sketch pad, and glowers at me. "Turn your head. Toward the lamps."

I turn. He chews his pencil, sketches, fusses. "No. Not that. Look at me, ugly thing."

I obey, but involuntarily I pull my lips back from my teeth. Anton stops drawing to stare, then smiles, delighted. "That expression. Hold that and don't move. Marvelous. Marvelous."

I hold still until my jaw aches. From the corner of my eye I see Angèlie get up from her play and toddle into the other room. A moment later she comes close to my chair with something in her mouth, gnawing lustily.

It's a human rib.

I break my pose to stare at her. She chews at the sawed bone with obvious relish, picking bits of muscle free with her tiny inexpert fingers and sucking them loose. The smell of the meat reaches me and saliva fills my mouth.

Grave meat. He's feeding her grave meat, and she's been here seven days. Angèlie sees me watching and pulls the rib from her mouth and waves it, grinning widely. Already her little teeth are becoming sharp.

Oh, no. Oh, no no no.

"I said she is not your business." Anton gets off his stool and palms my face, turning my head back. "You're a bit pale, Madame. Let me get you something."

He puts down his sketchbook and walks away into the other room. I rub my face and watch Angèlie, wondering what I'll tell Marie.

Eating dead flesh turns humans into ghouls. It's a long process in an adult, but a quick one in such a young child. Looking into Angèlie's face, I see why her eye color wasn't clear before: they're turning yellow.

This man knows what he's doing. He has to.

"Madame." Anton has returned with two glasses of opaque red wine: one brim-full, the other much less so. He hands me the fuller of the two; the smell of blood I'd noticed before is suddenly much stronger. "Please. It will put more color in your cheeks, and the contrast will be good for the canvas."

I hesitate. Ghouls tend to avoid spirits; the flavor they give to human flesh is as unpleasant as the sick feeling the next day. But he's watching me with uncomfortable intentness, and slowly I lift the glass to my lips and drink, swallow by swallow, grimacing at the gamy saltiness of vine's blood mixed with man's. When I hand him the empty glass, I'm hot-faced and breathing hard, and my stomach seems to have constricted around the mixture. "Much better already," Anton declares, and his mouth is cruel when he smiles. "Much better. Another glass?"

"No." I shake my head, and the sensation of it stays with me. "Thank you. No."

"We'll see." He sets the glass on the floor and takes to his stool again. "Now. Look toward the lamps."

I do as he says, wanting to spit. There are ten or fifteen lamps, clustered on one side of the room, and their flames flicker and dance, then start to sway. I blink rapidly, my heart pounding, but the effect doesn't disperse. The wine; he'd put something in the wine and used the blood to mask the taste, and it's working fast.

Angèlie. I can't see her. I have to get Angèlie and go.

"I'm sorry, Monsieur," I say—or I think I say it. My lips feel thick and tingly. "But I should—"

I struggle upright, but the floor reaches up for me.

✳✳✳

When I open my eyes, I'm in the second room.

I'm on the floor, propped up beside a half-butchered corpse, surrounded by a semicircle of lit lamps. My shawl is gone, and my arms are behind my back, my wrists tied with a piece of fabric.

The carpet is littered with dropped brushes, canvas scraps, sheets of stained paper.

"So." Anton stoops into my vision and pulls painfully at my feet, wrenching me into a sitting position. My head throbs. "My very own ghoul, just when I thought I'd have to grow my own." He pulls at my lips next, studying my teeth, then tips my head back. My neck aches with its weight. "Oh, I know what you are, just as I know who sent you. Did she think I wouldn't know that dress? She used to wear it for me."

Is this Marie's trap for me after all? I flex my hands sluggishly, trying to work saliva into my mouth, trying to breathe deeply and clear my head. I growl and spit, and Anton slaps my face, rocking me. "Now, Madame. I've been hospitable, have I not? Don't fret. I'll let you go soon enough." He reaches down into the ruined ribcage of the corpse, yanks a lump of flesh free from deep within, and pushes it into my mouth. "Chew." He taps my chin hard enough to click my teeth together. "Chew. I want to see blood on your chin."

He drags an easel near, a canvas already fixed in place, while I chew and collect blood in my mouth and let it leak from my lips. The meat, at least, isn't tainted like the wine. "It's not your fault Marie doesn't understand," he mutters. "I'll let you go, you go your way, no one has to get hurt. Only let me immortalize you first. Madonna and corpse."

He's going to kill me if I can't get away. I can see it in his eyes, despite his claim to the contrary. His smile is bright and crazed.

"Ma? Dada?" Angèlie toddles close to her father's feet and stumbles. He curses and picks her up, then eyes me and sets her in my lap, grabbing at my bodice and pulling it down, shoving Angèlie against my breast.

Angèlie grabs the fabric in both hands and bites hard into my flesh. I yelp and try to struggle away, but the pain of her teeth knifes through the fog in my head, and I tug harder at my bound wrists. "Angèlie, no."

She gnaws at skin and fabric. I whine, and Anton laughs

mockingly. "Oh, Madame, you're perfect." He takes Angèlie out of my lap and sets her on the floor, turning to his canvas. "Come. Let me make a masterpiece of you."

He reaches down for a tube of paint. I pull against my restraint harder. With a stab of pain, my left thumb dislocates, and my hand slips half out of the binding, loosening the cloth enough to pull myself free. I stagger up to my knees and into Anton, still off-balance from the drugged wine, but in his bent position the lunge is enough to knock him off his feet. He hits the floor, sending his easel tumbling, smashing half a dozen oil lamps. The carpet and canvas start to burn, then the paper catches, and he's head-down in the midst of it all.

I push to my feet. Anton screams and twists. His hair is burning, his shirt already half consumed. As he struggles to rise, I kick into his ribs and he falls back, breaking more glass, spilling more oil for the flames.

"Angèlie!" He'd set her down almost at his feet, and I snatch her up from the fire's edge hastily. She's whimpering and coughing, the hem of her dress oil-soaked and beginning to smolder. I kick the remaining lamps aside and dash through the spreading destruction, my boots stinking as the leather scorches, using my free hand to stamp out the little flames creeping up my skirt. Holding Angèlie, I try to work the door's multiple locks with only one hand, but I'm still too heavy-headed to be dexterous enough. Clumsily I tear a piece from my skirt, wrap it around my fingers and beat the glass from the window. By the time the gap is large enough, smoke is filling the room. I guide Angèlie through the hole, then force myself through after her.

Anton is still screaming.

I'm scraped, bitten, bleeding. I hit the ground hard, roll to my hands and knees. I work my thumb back into its socket and vomit into the snow. Then I haul myself upright, grab Angèlie, and break into a run.

Somehow, I get as far as Marie's front door before my legs give out.

***

I kneel in the snow for only a moment, panting and coughing, holding tight to Angèlie, who's gone quiet and solemn. Then I use the doorknob to pull myself up, and start to knock, but Marie's already opening the door.

"Angèlie!" Marie snatches her child from my arms and bursts into tears, whirling her around in a hug, weeping into her hair. "Oh, thank God, thank God, I thought I'd never—"

She's reaching for me too, but now she stops. "Delphine, what's happened? Why do you smell like smoke? Why are you bleeding?"

I clasp her arm and guide her back inside. I shut the door. "Anton's dead, Marie."

Marie's eyes widen, and then her expression collapses; she screws up her eyes, buries her face in Angèlie's hair, and says in a tiny voice, "This is true?"

I'd run from the house before the smoke had become obvious...but he had already been on fire. All that lamp oil... "It's certainly very likely."

Marie shudders, hugging her daughter; then she lifts her face and sniffs, and I can see her rapidly pulling herself back together. "It couldn't be helped," she decides. "Angèlie needs a bath and a change, and so do you. Come. Tell me everything."

***

I take only a wet cloth to wash off the blood and the grime; Marie has been thoughtful enough to wash out the clothes I'd first come with and hang them up to dry, and it's the change I'm most grateful for.

I tell her almost everything: the lamps and canvases, the drugged wine, the fire. Everything except seeing Angèlie gnaw on a rib from a corpse. Marie sees the results herself: she's grimly wiping oil paint from Angèlie's skin when she puts down her rag and peers down at her daughter's face. "Delphine, something's wrong with her eyes. The color's different, they should be blue..."

I look over her shoulder: Angèlie's eyes aren't yet yellow, but they're too light to be brown. The little girl smiles up at her mother, and Marie takes a step back. "Her teeth," she says faintly. "Delphine, what did Anton do?"

"He was feeding her flesh from the corpse." She's white. I take her shoulders and shake her. "He wanted to turn her into a ghoul. He said he was...trying to grow his own."

"That's not even possible." But Marie looks into Angèlie's eyes again, looks at her teeth. Her hands are shaking, but she takes a deep breath and sighs. "No. I see it's true. God, I loved a madman." She wipes her own face and swaddles squirming Angèlie in a large towel. "What's going to happen? She's back where she belongs now, she can eat normal food. Won't that reverse the change?"

"I've never seen that happen." I touch Angèlie's pudgy cheek with a finger and she snaps at me, then giggles. "It comes quickly in children."

"So I have to feed her carrion?" Marie demands. "Oh, that man is going to rot in *hell*."

That would certainly be fair, but I don't offer an opinion. I just want to go home and sleep for a week. "Bones," I say. "Give her animal bones. Chicken, beef. Leave them raw, but crack them so she can get the marrow. Get livers and hearts. A butcher will think you're simply making soup."

"A lot of soup," Marie agrees, angrily. "And will that be sufficient?"

"For now, yes." I caress the top of Angèlie's head, staying away from her teeth. "And when it's not, you know where to find me."

***

For a week, for ten days, I have peace. There are no funerals and no mourners. I eat, and sleep, and heal. There's no more snow.

On the morning of the tenth day, the chain across the mouth of the catacombs rattles just after sunrise. I get up, light a few small lamps, and hear, "Delphine? Delphine, are you awake?"

Marie's stage-whispering, but in this space the sound is amplified. "I'm here," I call back, my voice still hoarse from smoke and cold, and I climb the steps to the entrance. Marie stands there with Angèlie, both of them heavily bundled against the chill; Marie has a bag on her arm.

I hold out my arms, and Marie passes Angèlie over: the child is thinner-faced and more sallow than she'd been ten days ago. She's becoming ghoulish rapidly. Then I pull the chain up for Marie to stoop under. "It's warmer down here," I say. "Mind the steps."

At this level I've cleared the niches of bones and filled them with other things: clothes, trinkets, books, candles and lamps. Marie looks around curiously, but only for a moment.

"It's not getting better," she says bluntly. "I got beef bones. That helped for a few days, but now she doesn't want them. She's bitten women at church. Yesterday I went across town for a neighbor's funeral Mass, and Angèlie howled like a fiend to get to...you know." Marie's jaw tightens. "Delphine, I love my daughter. I know this isn't her fault. But I can't give her what she needs now."

Neither can I, I think. I know nothing of raising children, save what I've observed. But Marie's right; Angèlie will need meat now, ghoul's meat and bone meal, and above all she'll need privacy as she grows, for her change to work out away from prying eyes. "I'll need her things," I answer.

"I brought some of them." Marie sets the bag down. "I'll bring the rest soon." Her voice thickens. "And larger things, for later. I have to go; I've taken a job with a seamstress and I can't stay longer."

She embraces me suddenly. "Forgive my old spitefulness, if you can. I can never repay you, Delphine, never. Not for all of this."

"Just come see her, Marie. Often. So she won't forget you."

"Of course, of course." The town clock is chiming six; Marie wipes her eyes with a gloved hand. "Angèlie, be good for Delphine. Be very good." She kisses Angèlie's cheeks and her forehead. "I'll be back soon. Tonight. I promise."

I lead her back out of the catacombs. She hugs Angèlie a final time and then me again, weeping. "Tonight," she insists, and walks away.

I watch her go. She looks back often, until she's passed out of sight.

"This," I say to myself, "isn't how I ever expected to become a mother."

"Mama." Angèlie tugs my hair and stares at me with wide, serious eyes. "Mama go?"

"Mama will be back," I tell her. She'll need a place to sleep, I'll have to rearrange everything...but first things first. That last grave I'd opened should still be easy to get into. "Come, little one. Let's find your breakfast."

MUTUALLY ASSURED

WHEN I OPENED my front door to the man in black, who was propping my storm door open with his shoulder and holding a crisp black envelope in gloved fingers, my first thought was that it was far too early in the morning to be selling anyone anything. My second was that I'd mislaid my glasses in stumbling out of bed at seven-thirty and couldn't tell if his suit was pinstriped without squinting. And my third, very distinctly, was *oh, no hat and coat, it's January, he must be freezing—*

Oh. No wonder he was here. It had happened after all.

Let's just mutually agree to hire out hitmen for each other if we ever show signs of becoming our mothers, my best friend Kay had messaged me on ICQ. We'd both been in our mid-thirties then, both single, busy on opposite continents yet still finding time to grouse together about our aging moms and what we considered their far-ranging paranoias. I explicitly remembered grinning at my screen and gleefully typing, *Okay! I can get behind that.*

The man in black still stood there, saying nothing. I took the envelope from his fingers: glossy, with a red wax seal. That had been the signal Kay and I had agreed on, the signal that the time had come, that four decades later we were finally—gasp, shock, horror—turning into our mothers after all. Kay had texted me about it just last week: *Lila, I'm afraid it's getting close. I just asked the postman if he'd like a scarf to stay warm, and he's not even organic.*

This man in my doorway certainly was. In fact, I was pretty sure, if I squinted, that his lips were turning blue. This north wind had a bite, after all. I ran my thumbnail along the flap of my envelope, around the seal. There was nothing in it, of course—that wasn't the point—but curiosity made me stop myself from opening it. "I assume someone's held up the other end of the deal?" Kay and I had agreed on that, too. She'd be first to go; she was younger. It was only respectful. She must've called in on herself.

He reached into his coat. I tensed, which made my back cramp, but all he pulled out was an identical envelope, its seal broken. He put it in my other hand; it definitely wasn't empty. Tucking my own envelope between two fingers, I pulled this one open. Photographs. On paper. I hadn't realized people still did that. I wondered if anyone still used ICQ.

I edged out the topmost one. It was all I needed to see: the outstretched arm, the pool of blood. I'd made Kay that bracelet for her thirty-fifth birthday; I'd recognize it anywhere. So. It was time.

I stood back from the door. "All right. Come in."

The man in black finally blinked. "What? Why?" he asked, and I had to smile. Eastern European accent. Kay hadn't forgotten that detail either.

"Young man"—I winced; I sounded exactly like Mama had—"I am seventy-nine years old and I'm *not* dying on my front porch, nor in my robe, and it's nineteen degrees outside, so *kindly* come inside and let me change into something suitable before you catch your own death."

He blinked again, but when I turned away from the door, he followed. "I'll make coffee in a few," I said over my shoulder, and limped up the stairs, smiling, humming a little. Too bad I couldn't message Kay to thank her for saving me from myself. This was really what friends were for.

BLEEDTHROUGH

ONE

IT'S RAINING. LATELY it's always raining. You hunch into your tattered coat and pull the collar up; you're in a hurry.

***

"Curiosity." The psychiatrist is a cyborg, Shelley is almost sure of it: she can't put her finger on exactly what gives her the certainty, but it's there. Maybe it's the way he talks, the words coming out in a drawl that's probably meant to be reassuring but that instead gives the impression his speech is stoppered in his throat. He blinks too slowly, smiles too stiffly. Like now, when he's saying, "Well. That's one I haven't heard for this simulation package before. Of course, I suppose it comes down to curiosity in any case, but most people aren't so forthright about it."

"It's true. But I was the girl who liked books instead of boys. My grandmother gave me *Grimm's Fairy Tales* when I was three and I got hooked on horror stories." Shelley eyes him: white-haired, pink-cheeked, eyeglasses with silver rims, dimples placed appropriately. It's the face, she decides; he may have all sorts of biomechanics under that suit and lab coat, but it's his face that tells her he's not just meat anymore, the way his affable expression doesn't change with his inflections. He's altogether the picture of the friendly American country doctor from a century ago, if his smile were more relaxed and genuine. She lies back on the reclining seat that will be her space for the sessions, and immediately pushes forward to sit on the edge again. Just as well that VR suits are padded, when this thing is all cold metal and plastic and stiff angles, bits of it poking in uncomfortable places. "Look, I've done six prior Futurepast simulations, Dr. Bowman, and I've never needed a psych consult before. Don't tell me that's simply because of my 'curiosity'."

Bowman laughs and shakes his head, still a too-slow movement, leaning back in his chair. He tugs at those glasses with a plump hand. "No. No, please, don't be offended. It's standard for this simulation package; prior experience has taught us it's a good idea. People are usually a little disturbed afterwards. They want to talk." He swipes through a few screens on the tablet balanced on his knee: her Futurepast profile. "You tried the Narnia package last year and reported satisfaction with it."

Shelley looks away from his face, if only to keep him from seeing her roll her eyes. "It was pretty," she says grudgingly, gaze flicking from floor to ceiling of this cubicle and back again. Institutional grey, livened by a stripe of grass green halfway up and the Futurepast Technologies logo stenciled on the wall in darker malachite. No one comes to these sessions for the aesthetics of the building. "The animals were cute. Aslan was wonderful, very convincing. I mean, once was enough, it's a little too sweet after a while. But I'd heard of the stories and it was nice. And on sale."

"Yes, I have a note here that you've tried several promotional packages. Narnia. The Mars colony. Genghis Khan's Mongolia," Bowman answers blandly. He's watching the tablet screen, not her. "But you paid full price for this one."

"It was the only way to get in. That, and agree to the supervision." Shelley pulls her knees up as much as she can without leaning back. "Is there going to be a problem?"

Bowman lets out a slow breath. "It's just a little unusual, in my experience. Most of the people who've bought the Ripper simulation package have been historians, at least amateur ones, trying to puzzle out the killer. Sometimes law enforcement officials who want to try their hand at nineteenth-century detective work. Not—" He stops, and she can practically hear circuits straining as he ponders his approach. "I'm just a little concerned that you seem to be interested solely in the entertainment value." He makes eye contact with her for a second and looks back at the tablet. "You work for Arlington and Bond."

Shelley grimaces. Work, of course it's about work, she's dissatisfied with work and that's a *motivator*. "I'm in accounting. Telecommuting, the department got physically downsized last month." She still remembers the weight of the stapler she'd just picked up when Brian, her boss, had walked in with a hangdog apologetic look and told her that her physical presence onsite was no longer necessary. "It's been, well, it's been a change. I'm not stupid, I can balance the books in my pajamas while I'm eating Cheerios at the kitchen table. But it's not the same, especially with the twenty percent pay cut." She huffs. "All right, fine. Maybe I'm just a little frustrated and resentful. Maybe this is stress relief or therapy or something. Look, if this is going to be a problem I can just go back down to the front office and get a refund—"

"It's not a problem. It's not a problem." Bowman's voice has gone smooth and conciliatory and for a moment Shelley fears it's going to get stuck in that loop. "I just want you to be aware that this program does carry a degree of psychological risk, and—" He stops abruptly again, studying the tablet. "Here are your release forms, and your receipt. So apparently you do understand." The psychiatrist sounds almost disappointed. "And it looks like your measurements are already on file and your suit's ready. When do you want to begin?"

"Now." Shelley slides off the edge of the chair. "It's the end of August. I'd like to start now."

***

It starts like always: the sudden fogging of your vision, deep grey shot through with green, the sickly color of a tornadic sky. Then a sudden sinking feeling and the clearing of your vision and you're *there.*

✳✳✳

It's two in the morning.

Here in London you can always tell the unfortunates simply by their presence: no self-respecting woman of any means would be out on these streets at this hour. Tonight it seems every public house has at least two standing in the street outside, wearing probably everything they own but trying to give an air of shabby gentility to it: a lace shawl here, a fresh posy penned there, skirts drawn just so, catcalling every man they see. It's enough to make you jittery with possibility, but you focus on the presence and weight of the knife sheathed in your left boot and walk on: you have to choose carefully.

In Osborn Street you spot a young one, and sidle onto the Whitechapel Road corner to watch her. Pretty enough from a distance, in a pale sprigged dress that's been cunningly vented in the skirts to show a darker material underneath, a crocheted shawl hanging low on her shoulders; she has to be freezing at this hour of the morning, because the stammer in her voice when she beckons to passersby is part hesitancy and part pure shivering.

She looks round and catches sight of you. You watch her mouth work as she takes a half-step toward you and oh, she's so obviously new at this. You wonder how old she is—she doesn't look sixteen—and you touch the brim of your hat to her and smile, but shake your head. She's too much of an angel still: she's not at all what you want.

She might be missed. You can't have that. Not yet.

"Lookin' for someone, sir? Someone to keep you company a bit?"

You turn around. The woman who spoke is smiling at you, hands held boldly out; she's dark and petite, the top of her head perhaps just reaching your chin. The bonnet she's wearing is obviously new, just as the rest of her clothes are obviously not. You see a ragged hem, a patched sleeve. She's forty if she's a day and she exhales gin: she even sways a little where she stands.

She's perfect.

"Yes," you say. "Yes, I'd like that."

***

The fee she names is ridiculously small, the price of a night's lodging in Thrawl Street or any other hole. She calls herself Polly; it could be a hundred other things. You try to lead her, guide her to an appropriately dark place, but she's desperate enough for that small bit of coin that she drags you instead, stumbling twice in her drunken show of eagerness. By the time she's got you in a blind alley you've managed to work the knife out of your boot and into your hand, hilt up your sleeve, tip curled in your palm. It's uncomfortable, blade pressed into your forearm, but it won't be there long.

You keep your hands back and she doesn't see it; she's too busy working her fingers under your belt anyway. "Bit shy, eh?" She chuckles. "See that a lot. Well, don't you worry, lad, Polly will take care o' that."

Now. Now. You grab her shoulder, haul her around, tug her back against you and yank off her bonnet. A fist in her hair to get her throat back and you cut deep, as deep as you can, fast, one side and then the other. The scream she might have made comes out her sliced throat as a whistling bubbling spray of blood.

You drop the knife. Another hand to twist in the layers of fabric at her neck, to hold her up while she bleeds out. The spurts become oozes slipping down her neck into her clothes, rolling back toward her hair. When you let her go she hits the ground like a stone, and makes no sound.

She's face down. You find the knife and take it up and turn her over. You lift her skirts. Four layers. Three pairs of stockings. You were right. She's wearing everything she owned.

You draw her clothes up higher. Her belly is white and sunken, and the sight of her flesh does nothing to stir you. Still, it feels good to sink the knife beneath her navel, to pull and pull against the resistant flesh, to hear it part in a jagged line with the wet noise of a tearing bedsheet.

You leave her body in Buck's Row, with her skirts thrown up.

✳✳✳

An attendant helps Shelley out of the VR suit, sprays her naked body with rose-scented disinfectant and warm water, then towels her down briskly and gives her a papery grey bodysuit to pull on; her street clothes are in a locker in the changing station at the end of the hall. By the time Bowman comes into the cubicle, Shelley is perched on the edge of the seat, drinking water from a rice-paper cup. He leans in the doorway. "Hi. Feeling okay?"

"Fine. Fine." Shelley drains the cup and crumples it, twisting it in her hands, feeling it tear. *Like Polly.* "Jittery, maybe." She'd forgotten that from her last sessions. The adrenaline rush, the comedown, the sense of snapping back into the real world and finding it somehow *less* than the one she'd left. "But it'll be okay in a few minutes." For a split second, everything's garish, even the grey cubicle walls, too bright and too loud; then her senses recover and it's all plain again. She tosses the remnants of the cup at the wastebasket and misses, but the attendant is there for the rebound. "It was...easier than I expected. Fast."

Bowman watches her. "The experience?"

"The murder. He—I—it was just so quick. Like I'd planned it, and I don't even know where the knife came from." Another effect of VR: no prior 'memories', just dropping you into the world with what you need like a videogame. Shelley shrugs it off; she doesn't want a lot of prying questions about her feelings right now, even if it disappoints him. "We'll talk about it next time. Right now I just want to go home and shower."

✳✳✳

Shelley picks up her clothes at the changing station and trudges to the elevator, feeling grungy and exhausted and elated all at once, the neurochemical backlash of the VR experience setting in.

Fortunately the only other person in the elevator is a young blond man who looks like he might be twenty. He's a newbie: he's got that wide-eyed uncertain look, and a nametag stuck to his Springsteen T-shirt that says 'Erik'. His jeans are ripped at the knees to show red paisley cotton underneath, and bright pink earbuds trail to the candy-green iPod in his hand. When she steps into the elevator, his gaze shifts from the device to her. "Um. Hi."

It's said with a nervous tongue-lash of his lips. Shelley groans inwardly; she just wants to go home and clean up and balance a few accounts for work, not make small talk with this kid. "Hi. You're new at this, right?"

Erik blushes almost as pink as his earbuds. "Does it show that much? My brother talked me into this, he got a huge deal on the 'Twentieth Century Horror Authors' package. Says it's a real wild thing."

Shelley shakes her head; she's never even seen that in the catalogue. No wonder it's apparently cheap. "Talentless hacks who all died too young?"

Erik stutters a laugh. "Yeah. I guess. He says I should start with Lovecraft, says the dream sequences are awesome."

Dream sequences? For a moment Shelley wonders what she'd dream about in the simulation, if she stayed under long enough. "Sounds fun."

"I hope." He fidgets. "So. You doing a package too?"

She nods. "My seventh. Jack the Ripper."

"Oh. Cool." Erik shrinks into the corner just a little. "Um. Trying to find out who he was, or—?"

"Right now I don't give a damn who the killer was. I just wanted to try the murders." The elevator stops and Shelley hoists her bag. "I'm thinking of it as my vacation."

***

Polly.

Shelley thinks of her in the shower, washing off the last of the VR suit's tacky adhesive; and at her desk with a talk show droning in the back of the living room, plush smoky carpet under her bare feet as she digs her toes into the fibers and prods the Mancini account into correctness on her tablet.

The woman hadn't screamed; she hadn't had time. Her potential cries for help had come out as short-lived bursts of blood-laced air through the gaps in her throat, and yet the curiosity Shelley feels is muted, clinical and distant, as though she's watching a moth struggle as it's spitted on a pin.

A body spitted on a knife.

Later, in the kitchen, she oils her hands and makes meatballs from panko and ground turkey, dropping them one by one into a pot of simmering vegetable-laden sauce. Outside her front door she can hear clawing, whining, loud meows: her neighbor Elsa Dannoy has left her cat out again. Bruno, Shelley thinks, or something like that, a skinny orange thing that roams the complex because his owner isn't home enough to remember to keep him inside. Elsa has children in three adjacent states and she makes the rounds every week to each one of them.

She has the last meatball in her hand. The cat meows again and for a moment Shelley seriously thinks of throwing the meatball out to the animal, if only to shut him up. But she restrains herself: anything you feed becomes something that stays. Everyone knows that. She'll have to complain to the super again.

Someone to keep you company a bit?

Shelley thinks of Polly, of the quick sweet bite of the knife and the thick stickiness of blood not her own, and eats the meatball raw.

TWO

Shelley doesn't bother with a shower this morning: there's no point when she'll need one after her session anyway. It's a morning appointment today, so she just pulls on her old comfortable purple sweats and ties her hair back into a ponytail. She's just got her shoes on and grabbed a peach from the kitchen—scouting out the window reveals no sign of Mrs. Dannoy's cat, so she must be home for once—when her phone vibrates in her pocket.

She pulls it out and grimaces at the screen. Work. It's always work. "Hey there."

"Shelley? Brian." Not just anyone, of course, oh no, it's got to be the boss-man himself. "You busy?"

She gets her keys and jacket. "On my way out the door. Those Futurepast sessions I told you about? All week?"

Shelley says it with a hopeful please-leave-me-alone note in her voice, but Brian just answers, "Yeah. You mentioned that. I don't think it's smart, cramming a month's worth into a week like this, but it's your dollar."

All six thousand of them, Shelley thinks with a grimace. "Was the Mancini work all right?"

"It was great. Um." Brian suddenly sounds like Erik from last night. "I've got two more accounts that need to be done by tomorrow morning, I'm putting the email together now, and then. Um. That's going to be it for a while."

That's *what*? Shelley almost drops the phone. "That's going to be it? Brian, what the hell does that mean, are you running out of work for me or something? Cutting me loose?"

"...Yes." God, she can picture the way he ducks his head, that stupid apologetic look she'd seen before, like he's kicked someone's puppy. "I'm sorry, Shell, but you know the cutbacks come from higher up. Look, don't worry, your record's stupendous, I'm sure things will pick up soon."

"Brian. Stop. Just...stop." Shelley realizes she's gritting her teeth and forces herself to relax; her jaw aches. Fuck. "Look. I've got to go or I'll be late. I'll talk to you when I get the accounts sorted out, I don't have time to kill."

***

Time. No. You have other things to kill, perhaps, but not time. It's almost daylight.

The woman approaches you on Hanbury Street, just past number twenty-nine. She's a little taller than the last one, and not so overdressed: a little heavier, maybe, or at least stouter in the face, but the luster of her wavy dark hair in the beginning light of morning isn't without its charm, and she shows fine bright teeth when she smiles.

She smiles a lot and, well now, you're just the sort of gentleman she's looking for, aren't you, the sort who's surely got a few minutes for a good time with Annie if he don't mind spending just a bit of coin?

You don't mind, and say so. There's enough light now you can see her eyes are blue. She reaches up and catches you about the neck, as if she's about to kiss you. Instead she just tugs you down a bit to laugh in your ear and nudge you toward a nearby yard. "Right here. Inside the fence. Sixteen people in that house and they wouldn't know if you pulled it down round 'em. Be a dear and lift the gate for us."

Such a bold thing, and so very foolish. You reach down, but what you grab is the kerchief around her neck, slipping your hand under it. Twisting, twisting as she pulls at you, flails, a ring slipping off her finger. But she can't break your grip, especially not when you jam your free hand in under her chin and squeeze.

Twist. Squeeze. Her hand drops away from yours. Her face mottles. You let go, for a moment, reaching for your knife, and she falls back against the fence.

She's too far gone to strain for air, is poor Annie. You pull her head back where she's fallen and cut deep into her throat. Blood oozes: it doesn't pulse, just seeps out along the blade. The cartilage of her larynx crunches as it parts.

You lay her down. Past saving now, poor Annie, quite past saving. Now the deep work: pry the blade out of her throat, wipe it on the grass, shove it into her abdomen low and to the hilt. Quick drag, rent-cloth sound of flesh tearing, lower noises, liquid. Parting the wound shows viscera; you shove your hands in and draw it out in loops, pulled up over her shoulders. In the cool air she steams, a sparrow folded in the wings of her own flesh.

The sunlight is brightening and you're panting. You pull your knife free, wipe it clean on her skirt, turn her face to one side and stroke the wave of her hair.

***

There's a butcher shop, an honest-to-God butcher shop, on the route between Futurepast and Shelley's apartment. She hasn't stopped here in months, but she'd come out of her post-session shower thinking of her grandmother's chicken-liver ravioli.

It had seemed appropriate.

***

The fellow behind the counter at the butcher shop is an android, an old model, his face sculpted in synthetic flesh that's fixed in a mask of grim determination, his movements stiff and almost comical. He doesn't speak; Shelley keys in her order at the counter and waits, and in just a few minutes she's on her way home with a pound of fresh chicken livers in a plastic container, blood pooled in the bottom.

A chicken liver isn't exactly of the same order of palatability as a meatball, but in the kitchen, listening to Mrs. Dannoy's cat whine, she eats one anyway, wiping blood from her chin with a paper towel, studying the grainy toughness of the organ, the bitter iron taste like a handful of nails in the back of her mouth.

Hadn't the Ripper eaten parts of some of his victims? Bowman would know, but she's not going to ask him. She'd blown off the after-session talk because she hadn't felt like discussing Brian and having her motivations for these sessions brought up again.

It's a little morbid fun. That's all. Just a good time.

✱✱✱

Brian calls again while the ravioli is cooking, while Shelley's tapping at her tablet to re-sort spreadsheet columns. Parnett is the name on this account: her next to last piece of work for God knows how long. "Shelley? Look—"

"Brian, if you want this shit by in the morning, I'm busy." Tap. Tap.

"Look, don't be mad at *me*, I'm talking to management," he insists. "They'll—"

"Work something out?" Shelley rolls her eyes even though he can't see it. "Yeah. Sure. You look. Don't worry. I'll land on my feet."

At just that moment Mrs. Dannoy's cat lets out an enormous moaning meow. Shelley curses and nearly drops her tablet. "Jesus Christ," Brian says, "what was that?"

"Neighbor's cat," Shelley sighs. "She leaves home and leaves it outside. We've all complained and the landlord won't do anything."

Another wail. Brian winces. "Shouldn't you do something?"

"Yes. Check my ravioli." Shelley gets up. "It's against my better judgment, but maybe I'll feed it."

THREE

Oh, you've got yourself a posh one here. All genteel-like. Took your arm and walked you along while you talked the business. He didn't argue the price, even told you how smart you look—and of course you do, all this black, very sleek. He'd even given you the posy on your jacket, red rose and maidenhair fern.

He hasn't commented on your Swedish accent once. You're always a little wary of the men, that's just good sense, but this one almost makes you feel safe.

You don't mind when he pulls you into Dutfield's Yard. The Workers' Club is meeting across the street, even though it's after midnight, and you can hear them singing. People will probably come out to listen; it's lovely singing.

"On your knees." He says it gently.

Oh. So that's what he wants. Well, that never takes long and in this black outfit it's not as if anyone will see you—

Then he grabs your hair, and something's in your throat before you can scream.

***

"What the fuck!" Shelley's half out of the VR suit, pulling at the taped-on leads inside while the attendant tries to cover her with a towel. "Bowman, what the fucking fuck—"

"Shelley." Even his voice makes her want to punch him. "Shelley. Calm down. The program ran the wrong segment, that's all."

He makes it sound like it's her fault. She glowers and grabs at the towel. "Look." Brian's word—fucking Brian—but she forces evenness into her voice. "Look. Dr. Bowman. I've had enough lately. First I get downsized to telecommuting, then I have to deal with a goddamn pet-abandoning neighbor my landlord doesn't care about, and now I'm about to lose the job I *have* because there's not enough work for me." She looks him in the eye. "Don't spoil it, okay? Give me my damn catharsis."

"Fine." Bowman holds up his hands: ineffective, pathetic. "I'm sorry. I apologize unreservedly. Do you want to run the segment again?"

"No." Shelley lies back so the attendant can work her back into the suit. "No. Sorry, it's ruined. Go on to the next one."

***

You take the first woman you find in Mitre Square. By God, you were interrupted once; it's not going to happen again.

She's drunk like Polly had been, drunk enough to go along with you, and you can tell she's not a prostitute all the time—she's got a thimble on one finger and a needle in her collar. Probably her man's turned her out; the most you can get from her slurred rambling is that her name is Kate.

The southwest corner of the square is far enough. You've had practice: you seize her neckerchief and cut her throat, side to side, slicing her right ear as reflex makes her try to pull away. You drop her and she falls on her back. Her bonnet has slid backward. The thimble clinks on the stones and rolls away.

Her mouth is open. Half smiling. You cut it deeper. Throw her skirts up and her legs apart. Kneel. Remember the other one: blade in belly fat, sink it deep, drag across. Cut through the intestine: pull it out, cast it aside. Reach back to her left kidney, veiled in its caul of fat. Slice it out: a keepsake, an ornament. Perfect the work.

Your hands are shaking. She's still warm.

***

The cat wails.

Shelley had finished the last of her work with a bottle of red wine and the last of the ravioli. She's not talking to Brian, not now. Not anymore.

Another pitiful noise from outside, and she groans. Brian telling her she's out of work, Bowman fucking up her session, and above all this damned cat...

There's a bit of ravioli left. Shelley dumps it onto a saucer and opens her door. "Bruno?"

Bruno is receptive to the ravioli, and receptive to petting. He doesn't even object when she scoops him up in her arms.

***

The recyclers in each apartment are alternatives to standard garbage disposals, turning food scraps into fertilizer for the complex's gardens. Right now Shelley's is straining under a load of fur and skin and small bones.

The amount of usable meat on such a thin cat is negligible and gamy. Shelley chews and winces. Mrs. Dannoy really should have fed Bruno better, or at least more often.

But he makes for a passing sandwich.

FOUR

This one will take time. You don't care. This one is your masterpiece.

She reminds you of the girl you'd seen the first night: not quite such a child, but younger than the others and fair, with that same half-innocent look. Her name is—was?—Mary Jane Kelly. Or Marie Jeannette. She told you both.

Not that it matters now.

Her lodging at Miller's Court is a single room, lit with a single candle. No time to waste in preliminaries: you'd paid her fee, thrown her across the narrow bed and sliced her throat back to her spine. It's easy now, after all your practice. Force her head aside. Bare her throat. Cut deep, deeper, watch the blood pulse out against the wallpaper.

Hold her down until it stops. Bathe your hands in her spray. Lick it clean.

You need more light, so you cut her dress off methodically, wad the scraps into the fireplace, set them alight.

And you peel her.

Eyebrows. Ears. Roll her neat breasts in your hands and cut them away. Filet her: work the skin from her arms in strips, from her thighs in flaps, detach red muscle, dig down to white bone. Slice her cheekbones flat, scratch lines into her lips and let them drain.

Put your mouth to the gape of her throat and drink. To the

bared fibers of her pectorals, and chew.

Empty her. Up and down, side to side. Lungs. Liver. Kidneys. Lift. Pull. Draw the knife. Pillow her head on her discarded flesh. Take the meat in butcher's cuts from between her ribs.

Cut again. Gash her nose, her feet, her fingers. Always cut. Slip your blade into tenderest skin and lift her eyelids away.

This is not murder, not anymore. Not when you are gloriously fed and yet more gloriously bloodied, and she is cooling, slippery, marvelous and inviting in her emptiness.

You've made a set of them, haven't you, from Polly to Mary Jane, these soiled doves cleansed by the kiss of your knife. Each one more complex, more pure, and this one is the zenith, the last work and the greatest.

No, this is not murder. This is art.

***

The only consequence to the cat's disappearance had been Mrs. Dannoy posting HAVE YOU SEEN THIS PET notices on every free surface and the landlord posting warnings about too much animal protein in the recyclers. Shelley can't think of it without giggling.

She dresses slowly once she's out of the VR suit: slowly, because she's still tacky with adhesive from the various leads in places only a good hot shower will reach, and stretching the skin there is uncomfortable, more so when the fabric of her thin black sweater and jeans both immediately stick into place. Slowly because she's dry-mouthed even after three bottles of water, because she'll start shaking uncontrollably if she doesn't try to keep her adrenaline load at bay, slowly so she won't dislodge the razor blade she'd tacked into the wrist of one sleeve.

She breathes deeply.

In the examination cubicle—still grey, still sterile, but with a tiny window and a better seat—she wipes her face and hands with a damp towelette and manages, for Bowman, a reasonably sincere smile. She stands; the psychiatrist settles onto his wheeled stool with a squeak of springs. "Well, that's that. How are you feeling?"

"Tired," Shelley admits, if it's possible to *be* tired while she's thrumming with sick anticipation, and adds to herself *and a little disappointed it's over, but I guess I can dream.* "It's been"—*fun, so gloriously bloodily fun*—"cathartic, I think. Sort of cleansing. I've definitely got a new perspective." She stretches, long and exaggerated, working the blade into her palm. The faint prick of it in the soft skin between her fingers is wonderfully familiar. "But right now I think I want to go home and enjoy my catharsis with a talk show and some cookies." She smiles. "I may even get my official resignation in on time."

"You certainly don't seem to be suffering any ill effects." Bowman blinks that annoying low-shutter-speed blink again. He's making notes into her file on his tablet. "For which I really do have to congratulate you. That's—"

"Unusual for this package," Shelley finishes, getting to her feet and making a show of stretching again. "I know. Like I said. Cathartic." She waits till his attention is back on the tablet, and steps in much closer, hands on her hips. "I'll admit, I've always wondered who decorated this place."

"What?" Bowman glances up, eyelids lifting from mid-blink into an approximation of mild annoyance. "Oh. Yes, it's...let's say, unfortunately plain. The Futurepast staff had the building painted before anything was ever moved in. You're far from the first person to notice, but they have a suggestion kiosk downstairs."

"I'll drop something in." She has to make him turn his head. For a moment Shelley thinks of Annie, just seized and whipped around, but she settles for hanging over his shoulder a bit and pointing at the blank wall behind him. "I mean, look at this wall. Nothing. Not even a stripe or a logo." She can feel his displeasure as he shifts, but he finally turns to look. "Now work with me a second. Just imagine..."

Shelley grabs his shirt collar and twists hard.

"...something red."

✳✳✳

Bowman doesn't taste like Mary Kelly had.

He'd been a cyborg after all: she'd found a respiration controller behind his thyroid, its titanium-coated carbon fibers winding up toward his brain in silvery threads under the muscles of his neck. Unlike his flesh, they refuse the edge of her blade.

His meat is slick and oily, sweet with a chemical tang, lacking even the faint gaminess of Elsa Dannoy's tough, stringy cat. By the time Shelley gets to the elevator she's faintly queasy, but that's just the adrenaline talking.

There will be consequences, of course. She quickens her pace to match her pulse. No getting around that. There are always consequences, even if there have always been killers who've managed to fall through the cracks.

The only person in the elevator is the blond boy she'd met on the first day. Erik: factory-ripped jeans and a black T-shirt, but he's still got his iPod and newbie nametag. He gives her an uncertain, watery smile. "Hey, you're the Ripper lady."

"Yeah. I never introduced myself, did I? I'm Shelley." He's twitchy. Shelley glances down: anything? Anything to give her away? Blood under her fingernails, piece of Bowman between her teeth? She doesn't see anything out of the ordinary, not in these black clothes, so she gives him the brightest smile she can muster with her heart trying to hammer its way out of her chest. "Just finished up, and let me tell you I'm pretty beat. How about you and the horror-writer program, have you summoned Cthulhu yet?"

She says it teasingly, but Erik jerks and shudders. "Twice. Sorry, it—sometimes it gets to you a little, doesn't it? Like it's too real, too fast. I keep *dreaming*." He pulls his earbuds out and drapes the cord around his neck, fidgety, grimacing. "So. Um. You ever find out who your killer really was?"

Somewhere above, an alarm is sounding. Shelley leans against the wall of the elevator and closes her eyes.

—*Here in London you can always tell the unfortunates simply by their presence: no self-respecting woman of any means would be out on these streets at this hour. Tonight it seems every public house has at least two standing in the street outside, wearing probably everything they own but trying to give an air of shabby gentility to it: a lace shawl here, a fresh posy penned there, skirts drawn just so, catcalling every man they see. It's enough to make you jittery with possibility, but you focus on the presence and weight of the knife sheathed in your left boot and walk on: you have to choose carefully.*

You're on Osborn Street again, and again the tow-headed girl catches your eye, but this time you get a good look. Pale blonde, willowy, and she's changed her dress, blue calico skirt arranged just so, velveteen neckerchief tied around her throat. Beneath the carefully arranged fringe of her hair she looks up at you, eyes wide and blue, the set of her painted mouth uncommonly bold. She makes an offer without saying a word.

Not so much the angel, now.

Something's changed.

She's ready.

You smile, and bow, and hold out your hand—

"It was me," Shelley says with finality. "All along. Just me."

A SPOT OF BLOOD

I'VE JUST REACHED for the bleach bottle, my fingers tight on the cap, when she closes her hand around my wrist.

"Hold up, baby girl. What's this here?"

She shifts her grip to under my arms and pulls me upright. I'm myopic enough from my time bent over the half-butchered corpse in the bathtub that the blot on the floor wobbles in my vision for a second before it resolves, and I feel the press of her covered boots against the outsides of my own.

A single spot of blood between my feet, between hers. She takes the back of my neck and squeezes hard, forces my head down and holds me there. "Now, baby girl, we've talked about this."

And we have, but never about the things I've done right: how small-caliber rounds rattle around in the skull and don't come out; how to accommodate the way the carotids can hide when the head's pulled back; how to unfold plastic sheeting so it doesn't even crinkle. For Christ's sake, I'm wearing three pairs of nitrile gloves right now.

No, it's always the other things: the cut that isn't deep enough, the noise that isn't muffled properly, this single drop of blood on a bathroom floor.

I reach blindly for the bleach. "I'll take care of it."

"Honey, I don't think you realize how serious this is." She presses on my neck. "We don't leave traces. You know what I say about mistakes."

"Mistakes get you caught," I mumble.

"Damn right. And how many is this?"

She shakes me like a dog shakes a stuffed toy. I can feel my own carotids pulsing as I try to think.

"Two...no...three."

"And one I can forgive. Maybe two. You've been learning," she says. "But not this one, missy, oh no."

She lets go of my neck and grabs my hair, plastic cap and all, and yanks me to full height, spinning me around. The movement is dizzying. My vision swims.

When it clears, I'm looking out the open bathroom doorway down the hall, toward the kitchen. Two drops. Three. Dozens. Maybe hundreds.

I've left a blood trail.

She rips the surgical mask from my face. The elastic snaps. I whimper.

"You do the crime, chickadee, you're damn sure gonna do the cleanup. And this time, you're doing it the hard way."

When she shoves me, I fold, topple straight down on my knees. She plants the toe of one boot in my side. "I warned you how it would be. Now get started."

Knees burning, eyes watering into my safety goggles, I bend my face to the floor and start to lick.

PATIENT 49

IT'S THE SECOND DAY.

His name is Henry. He has to tell himself that, when a snatch of thought swims up through the fuzz. His thin cotton uniform is stained and blue and says only 49, but his name is Henry.

He had another electroshock treatment this morning. Doctor Haskins says the treatments will make him better, will help the—spasms?—*seizures* stop, though all he remembers of the experience is the dampness of the pads clamped to his temples, the sudden jolt that fills the back of his mouth with the taste of iron and feels like being struck between the eyes with a fluff-covered mallet. They leave a lot of blank spaces, the treatments, and the spaces only fill back up slowly.

He sits on his bed, which is bolted to the wall. The sheets are white and coarse. The room is all concrete, clean-scrubbed, walls and floor and ceiling, and from here he can see all of it. Desk: a concrete slab built into the opposite wall, and a chair. He hasn't tried the chair; nailheads stick out of the seat, and the frame looks splintery. Sink and naked pipes, but no mirror, because mirrors can mean glass shards and cutting. Shower and toilet in short open-faced stalls. Drain in the middle of the shower floor, surrounded by something that looks like rust but which he suspects is not, but his cotton-wool brain is too afraid to conjure the word for what it might be.

Iron bars in a cut-out square in one short wall, and no glass, because it rained last night and he sat up shaking in his blanket against the thunder, watching the water run down the wall and pool on the floor. Door in the other wall, steel door through which Doctor Haskins comes every day, steel door slightly ajar because he can go out if he wants, but the idea terrifies him. Outside is people and noise, and the darkness in his head, and *not knowing*. There are no clock and no calendar. The sky, through the barred square window, is dead white.

The room is eleven steps wide and sixteen steps long. He knows this. He walked it this morning when he was brought back from treatment. He counted. It made him feel better, counting. It was something he could hold onto.

There's something in the pocket of his shirt. Big black 49 on the back of the shirt, small black 49 on the front pocket. There's something in the pocket and he takes it out: a brown stone, oval, flattish, bigger at one end than the other and very smooth.

Someone gave him this. It could not have come out of the concrete.

Henry holds it in his hands and tries to remember. His head aches; his hands ache, though the stone is warm and silken. Someone had—

Yesterday.

✳✳✳

It's the first day.

He can't remember the name of the woman who had brought him here this morning, though her eyes had been blue and soft and kind. Sister? Wife? Does he have a sister or a wife? *Things will be better soon, Henry*, she had said before she'd walked out of his room, but everything else beyond that scrap of sound eludes him. Jean? Joan? June? *Jean*, he decides, maybe, but he can't be sure.

Right now he doesn't remember his own name, either. He doesn't remember why he's here. The *where* is equally a mystery, though *psychiatric hospital* flits through his mind and whisks away like a goldfish. Someone had taken him away for the first treatment and someone else had brought him back, but their faces are blurs he can't conjure. He lies on the bed and stares at the ceiling and sees nothing. His mind is fuzz and wool and soft-edged warmth, an abyss, a void, a sponge that can't hold water.

"You the one they brung in this morning?"

The voice is soft and sudden, and it makes some deep instinct bring him to his feet, his heart thudding, his nails biting his palms. Standing brings nausea and he stumbles, coughs, pitches forward into huge cold hands. There is a long blank moment and when it breaks, he realizes someone has held him over the toilet so he could vomit. His stomach clenches on emptiness as he's pulled back and set down on the floor.

"You catch your breath, now." The toilet flushes. His chin is lifted and his mouth wiped with something wet and soft, and abruptly the patterns click back into place. He is sitting on the floor and a huge dark man is stooped over him: bald, scarred, his uniform numbered 37 straining across broad shoulders. The man smiles and is missing teeth. "Better. What's your name, son?"

It's...49. He knew that before he came here, didn't he? But he starts to say the number and feels a broad finger beneath his lips. "No," says the black man numbered 37. "Real name. Before. You think, now."

Think. That's what the treatments are for, the thinking. He's bad at thinking. Everything goes dark. Fractures. He tries, feeling his eyes start to twitch, and closes them. Before. There was a before. "...Henry."

"Henry. Good." The black man squats so they're more even in height. "John Henry."

"No." Shaking his head hurts. "Just—"

"Henry. I know. Good name. Still. John Henry. Steel driver." Another gapped smile, and the black man pulls him upright. "I'm

Russell. Big Russ, room down the hall. This 37 don't mean nothin'." Once Russ is standing, his large hands tremble. "They say I got the nerves real bad, but I still got a name."

Russ slaps his numbered pocket, looks thoughtful for a second and reaches into it. He pulls out a brown oval rock, puts it in Henry's hand. "My granny called this her worry rock. Ol' river rock. You rub it, real nice an' smooth, talk to it, put your troubles in it, Granny always said. Helps a lot in a place like this. Me, I just look out for the new arrivals."

There are footsteps in the hallway. Russell guides Henry back to his bed and pushes him down gently. "Best I'm goin' on. They don't like catchin' you out o' your room here, but you in a good place. You give your troubles to that ol' rock an' get some rest, John Henry."

***

It's the third day.

He's found a faint green streak in his stone, and this delights him. Out of the mind-fog that follows treatment, he has named the stone Jade, though he doesn't know why; the word connects to nothing in the furry blank of his mind.

But in Henry's eleven-step-by-sixteen-step world, this pleases him too.

***

It's the sixth day.

During the day Henry keeps Jade in his pocket, though he's learned to hide her under his pillow—he doesn't know why *her*, but his mind insists—when Doctor Haskins comes in, or when he's taken out of his room for meals. He hasn't told the doctor about Jade. If anyone knew, he thinks, they would take her away, and the thought brings a strange shaking terror.

At night he strokes her, whispers to her, when the blanks of his mind begin to fill in and he has things to tell again. Memories. That's the word. Memories.

I had a job, before. Shoe salesman. I have a sister who looks like me.

His sister. Henry knows she looks like him, but he can't envision his own face. He runs his fingers over his skin—bushy eyebrows but thinning hair, long nose, slender lips, but no cohesion, no clear image—and tries to remember her name again and fails, and not knowing makes his hands shake.

At night, when it rains—and it always seems to be night to him, when it rains, but maybe that's just inside his head—he puts Jade on the edge of the window with iron bars and no glass. He isn't a tall man and it's a stretch, but he lets Jade be washed by the rain, lets his secrets be washed out with her.

And this, too, pleases him.

✳✳✳

Somewhere, between shocks, he loses track of the days.

✳✳✳

When Henry opens his eyes, he's on the concrete floor beside his bed. A woman in a white cap stares down at him as she empties a syringe into his arm. He screams, weakly, and tries to turn away, but his back aches and his hands are clawed, and his clothes are wet.

"...not working like I'd hoped." The words, tinny and muffled, come from a man standing behind the woman, a thin balding man in a white coat. Doctor. Doctor...the name won't come. "I think he's going to need surgery."

✳✳✳

Later, after Henry's been redressed, after he's slept off the sedative and been given water, the doctor comes back. Doctor Haskins: the name is embroidered on his white coat. Haskins smiles and pulls up the rickety-looking chair, and Henry reaches under his pillow to brush Jade with his fingertips. She's cold and soothing. He doesn't trust this man with the coat and the lined worn face. He doesn't trust the chair.

"You've had two weeks of electroshock treatments, Mr. Dillard," Doctor Haskins says. "Your seizure episodes have decreased in frequency a little, but not in severity. Not as much as I'd hoped, anyway. Your memory's affected, you're not retaining things, you don't vocalize properly. The nurses say you never talk." He shifts his weight and the chair creaks. "For the sake of giving you a chance at normal life, I think surgery will have to be our next option."

Seizure. Frequency. Severity. Those words fall through the sieve. *Surgery*: that sticks. Surgery on his brain. Henry has to work saliva into his mouth, and concentrate hard. "Will it hurt?"

"No." Haskins puts a hand—warm, leathery—on his shoulder. "It won't hurt. You won't even remember it." His voice is gentle, and Henry feels reassured. "The procedure's called a transorbital lobotomy. We'll do it in the morning."

***

It's the fifteenth day. Henry knows because he's asked.

He's taken from his room early and put into a wheelchair, pushed down a dull gray corridor he doesn't recognize into a room he's never seen. He's guided onto a draped metal table and pushed down flat, and hard leather straps are fastened around his wrists and chest. Doctor Haskins is standing at the head of the table, and Henry rolls his eyes up to the doctor questioningly, mutely.

"You'll be fine, Mr. Dillard." Haskins is wearing gloves, and holding a thin metal instrument in one hand. "We just need to keep you still. That's all."

He bends, and his shadow falls over Henry's face, and everything fragments.

***

"How are you feeling, Mr. Dillard?"

He opens his eyes and blinks heavily. Nothing will focus: the voice tickles some faint bell of memory, but the face is a smear. His vision twitches back and forth; his tongue feels thick and furred. "...Hurts."

"Don't worry. You may have a headache for a few days, but your surgery went splendidly." Something creaks. "Can you try to stay awake? I just want to ask a few questions."

His eyelids feel massive and swollen. A word. He needs a word. "Y...yes. Try."

"How old are you?"

"...Thirty."

"And what year is it?"

"Nnn." So easy to just keep his eyes shut, to slide into oblivion. "N-nineteen. Fifty. F-five..?"

"Very good. Mr. Dillard?"

No. Quiet. Sleep. Something leaks from his right eye and is wiped away with a piece of gauze.

"Mr. Dillard?"

He drags his eyes open. The right one leaks again and is wiped again. The gauze is a white blur streaked with red. "...Who?"

***

Days pass, all blank, unnumbered.

***

The blanks are filling in.

Since the surgery, the treatments have stopped, the ones that left his brain soft and liquid and empty. There have been other things since, bitter pills without the needles, without the shock that feels like nothing. The man in the white coat talking to him, pouring things in, filling the holes. Sometimes the new thoughts feel real, solid, like things that have happened; sometimes they're vaporous, twisting in his grasp, but still better than the nothingness of six weeks ago.

His name is Henry. He knows that now, and stands straight for it. Someone had called him John Henry once as a joke, but that was a long time ago and he doesn't remember the man's face or his name, only a steadying hand on his shoulder and a tooth-shaped gap in a smile.

And Jade. He still has Jade. He remembers her.

He sits on the bed with Jade closed in one hand, waiting. Waiting and listening. She's listened to so much.

"You're improving," the man in the white coat had said—this morning? Yesterday? "Your seizures have stopped, at least for now. Maybe they won't start again. As for everything else, I think with time, it'll all come back. Another week or two, Mr. Dillard, and I think you might go home."

He doesn't know why the man keeps calling him Mr. Dillard. His name is Henry.

But Henry had heard that, and told Jade as soon as he could, cradling her, hands shaking a little as he stumbled over the words. Out. Away. Improving.

Home.

He doesn't remember *home*: doesn't remember place or people. He's been too far away, too sick, too long. His stomach twists at the thought of a family, of a job, of more faces that blur and names that slip through his fingers, yet the word nestles in his mind in a little niche of comfort.

He sits on the neat white bed and strokes Jade's smoothness, whispers to her the last of his fears. Then he gets up and makes the stretch to push her onto the windowsill, not too close to the edge, because someone else might need a friend. A listener. It's looking out for the new arrivals. Henry wishes he could remember who'd told him that.

Then he takes up his seat on the bed's edge, arms folded, head down, and waits.

Home. He hopes he'll like it.

***

It's the forty-ninth day.

"I can't." Jean Dillard doesn't watch as Henry is shuffled back into his room; she can't stand his glassy stare, or how he fumbles to say even a single word. Instead, she stuffs her fists into the pockets of her long coat and turns on Doctor Haskins. "I can't take him home like this. I can't give him the care he needs. You said the surgery would make things better!"

"And it will," Haskins says soothingly. "The healing process just takes time, Miss Dillard. Give him six or eight months and you'll see a great improvement. Without the seizures, without the neurological burden, with a special therapist for his verbal deficit...your brother can dress himself, he can feed himself—"

"*That* is not my brother!" Jean wheels away to face the wall, clenching her jaw. Her blue eyes are flinty, and when she speaks, her voice is choked.

"I remember the day Henry had his first seizure. I was twelve. He was ten. Our father worked at a textile mill and he'd made us kites out of yellow silk scraps. We were flying our kites up on the hill behind our house, and Henry's got away. He was running after his kite and just—" She pauses, mouth working. "He cried, later, when he remembered he'd lost that kite. And as much as I've hated seeing him suffer all these years, at least I always knew he was still in there somewhere. But now you've just cut the kite string. That's all. You haven't helped him catch the kite, Doctor. You've just cut the string."

He puts a hand on her arm. "Miss Dillard—"

Jean shakes him off. "No. I can't. I can't. Maybe in a month or two, when I can see real improvement, but not now."

She smiles bitterly, her mouth a thin tight line. "Tell him I'm sorry."

***

When Doctor Haskins comes back into Henry's room, the pretty lady isn't with him. Henry frowns, clutching Jade in both hands, and says guardedly, "Home?"

The doctor winces. "No, Mr. Dillard. Not today, I'm afraid. Change of plans. But soon, I promise you."

"Oh." Henry nods limply and looks down, keeping his eyes on Jade. "All right."

He doesn't hear anything else Doctor Haskins says, or hear him leave the room; he's already forgotten the man. Henry's thinking of the lady, and the blue softness of her eyes. He'd had a sister once, he thinks, that had looked like her.

He wishes he could remember her name.

BONE DEEP

FOR THE FIRST time in weeks, I'm alone in the house. Gran's out talking over the garden wall with one of the neighbors; Mam's hanging out the wash. Me, I'm sitting on my bed with our best kitchen knife, running the edge over the hard points sticking out beneath my fingernails. It should hurt, but it doesn't; the skin parts just a bit, bloodlessly, and there's the grating sound of metal scraping bone.

I press harder.

It started six weeks ago last Sunday, the day after I turned fifteen. When I went to bed that night, it was insidious, a little niggling almost-itch behind my kneecaps and in my wrists. But my knees swelled under my skirt when I trudged dutifully to school the next morning, and writing notes in my lectures just made fire blaze down my right hand in waves. The next day, it was both hands. Within a week, I was sneaking aspirin from the kitchen cabinet in handfuls, stuffing them in my skirt pockets, biting down on the bitter discs so I wouldn't sob from the searing ache that was twisting me inside out. I did that at home, at night, into my pillow.

It took Mam a full ten days to notice: "Ellie, you've shot up like a poplar."

She didn't smile. She grimaced instead, and backed me up against the edge of the half wall between the kitchen and the dining room, plopping the family Bible against the top of my head and marking the paint with a pencil before fetching the measuring tape. "Five feet and eight," she pronounced, wide-eyed, when she pulled the tape away. "Are you taller than me?" Mam demanded, and crowded so close my nose touched between her eyes. "Jesus, you're taller than me. And since the first of the month, too." She turned to look over her shoulder at Gran. "Is this normal?"

Gran shrugged, mouth tight around her cigarette. "Some girls get their height early, all at once. I did." She stood five foot four in bare feet.

It was Gran who sat at my bedside that night, patting my aching hands and balancing ice packs on my oversized knees. "Growing pains," she said, though her gaze narrowed as she eyed the length of my legs. "Best to get it out of the way now. Don't worry, it'll be over soon."

But in the night I woke screaming, my shift spotted with blood. My ribs had expanded and grown sharp-edged, breaking my skin from the inside. Mam yanked the fabric up and stared at me while Gran sponged me off with stinging alcohol, and this time there wasn't puzzlement in my mother's eyes. There was fear.

The doctor they took me to the next morning glanced at my knees and hands and ribs, took some measurements and jotted notes, muttered to himself and gave Mam a prescription for something with codeine in it, and never said a word directly to me. Growth spurt, he called it, and mumbled something about long bones and inflammation of the growth plates. It would pass, he said. That was the end of it.

That afternoon the pain in my knees came back, jabbing and twisting, so bad I could almost see my shins bowing inward. So I begged Mam for one of the pills, but she only said, "Not yet. Let's see how you are after school tomorrow."

I woke up next morning with my mouth throbbing. My cheekbones strained the contours of my face; I could see fissures forming in the skin. My teeth had become longer; my lips stretched when I formed a bite. Mam measured me again. I was another three inches taller. Gran looked up at me and whispered, "Swear to God, her bones are growing out of her."

I could barely get out of bed that day, despite hanging over it. There was no school. There was no school ever again.

The next week kept me changing, growing. My neck stretched with crackling noises. My jaw and elbows locked and loosened at odd times. Going through the doorways in the house meant bending nearly double, sleeping on my bed took folding myself in half, and the biggest shoes Mam could buy only fit on my feet a few hours. Gran crossed herself and swore and fed me aspirin, codeine, whiskey. None of it touched the pain. I lay on the floor and howled till the neighbors' dogs barked.

This morning, Mam needed a stepladder to measure me, and her tape wouldn't reach in one stretch. Six feet. Seven inches. I watched tears roll down her face as I tried to steady my too-long, agonized legs, and felt the ceiling against the top of my head.

Now I sit on the end of my bed, legs mostly in the floor, and I draw the knife over my fingertips again. They split entirely, and it's relief enough to make my eyes water. Tentatively I press the knife point into my thigh, where the outline of my femur is broad and plain, and push in. My skin rips with a noise like tearing tape, and there's no pain, no blood, only a release of pressure that makes me stuff my bulging knuckles into my too-wide mouth. Only a great glistening white expanse beneath the stretched crepe of my skin.

Gran was right. My bones are growing out of me. I take a few breaths and stick the knife in again.

If they want to escape, I'm setting them free.

SAY (PART II)

TRULY? YOU TRULY do not know how I came to be in this cell?

Say this, then.

Say that I killed him: say that I opened his throat with my singing blade and painted the kitchen walls crimson because he'd dared to look upon another. Say that I held him in my lap as he gurgled out the last of his air beneath wet uncomprehending eyes. Say I was arrested there.

Or say I found him in his garret on a filthy urine-damp mattress, already blue and frigid, the tourniquet on his arm and the needle still in the vein. Say I stroked his hair once, and kissed his forehead, and crept away.

Say I did both those things. That two timelines diverged and they are separately, equally true.

Or neither is.

Say he left me in September, which is true in every past, and I drank a bottle of Maker's Mark over the kitchen sink and trod the glass to shards under my bare soles so he might follow my bloody footprints home. Or say, perhaps, it was my own breath I laid bare on the edge of the knife, my own vein I tied off, my own mattress I fell across. Say that the walls were, nevertheless, painted.

Say the needle was in vain and the kiss of the blade sank none too deep, so that I breathe, so that I keep breathing. Say these things did happen, will happen, are happening, a spiraling maze of all possible outcomes, birth and death and love and blood. There is always blood.

Say you want to tilt my head and kiss my scars. The guards will let you in. There is nothing in this place sharper than a sigh, nothing sharper than the curve of your lip, nothing, nothing at all.

Except.

Only say that you wish to sit beside me. Say you've come to drink of what has passed and what will come. Do not be afraid. There will always be blood.

Say you will come in. Say that you will never be afraid. Say you were never afraid. Say that for this future, this past, this now, we will sharpen our teeth on each other.

You look like him, in this light.

Come. Say you'll let me taste you.

PUBLICATION HISTORY

(First publication only.)

"Half-Past." Ladies of Horror Flash Project, September 2019.

"Black, Red, Black." Ladies of Horror Flash Project, October 2019.

"Strong as Marble, Warm as Blood." Ladies of Horror Flash Project, August 2019. (warning: mention of nonconsensual sex)

"Itsy Bitsy Spider." Previously unpublished.

"Tempest." *Cthulhu Haiku II: And More Mythos Madness*, Popcorn Press, October 2013.

"Zero Hour." Originally published as "Patient Zero." Pen of the Damned, October 2019.

"And Drown Melancholy." *Morpheus Tales #27*, October 2015.

"The Lure of Light." *The Haunting of Lake Manor Hotel*, Woodbridge Press, April 2016. (warning: child death)

"Little Reaper." A Damned Halloween (Pen of the Damned), October 31, 2018.

"Hattie's Ghosts." This version published in *The Sirens Call #41* (Halloween Screams and Other Dark Things), October 2018. Originally published in *A Shadow of Autumn*, independently published, September 2015.

"Flycatcher." Pen of the Damned, August 2019.

"Ashes." Pen of the Damned, May 2018.

"Showroom." Ladies of Horror Flash Project, July 2019.

"Seeing Shadows." *Sanitarium* #50, November 2016. (warning: child death)

"Inhale, Exhale." Pen of the Damned, October 2018.

"The Tomb Wife." *Zen of the Dead*, Popcorn Press, October 2015.

"A Kiss of Flesh." Ladies of Horror Flash Project, March 2019. (warning: child death, cannibalism/necrophagia)

"Incision." *Cthulhu Haiku II: And More Mythos Madness*, Popcorn Press, October 2013. (warning: mutilation)

"Clary Recollected." *Possessions 3*, Third From the Right Productions, August 2017. (warning: child and domestic abuse, graphic depictions of violence, cannibalism)

"Radiance." Damned Words 35 (Pen of the Damned), November 2018. (warning: suicide)

"Say (Part I)." Originally published as "Say," Pen of the Damned, May 2019. (warning: drug overdose/suicide)

"The Sepulchre Bride." *Lupine Lunes*, Popcorn Press, December 2016.

"Baby." Ladies of Horror Flash Project, April 2019.

"Gravechild." *Lupine Lunes*, Popcorn Press, December 2016.

"Mutually Assured." Originally published as "Mutually Assured Destruction," *Once Upon a Crocodile* #3, May 2018.

"Bleedthrough." *Sanitarium* #29, January 2015. (warning: graphic depictions of violence, animal death, cannibalism)

"A Spot of Blood." Pen of the Damned, March 2019. (warning: D/s dynamics/unequal relationship)

"Patient 49." *Thrice Fiction* #23, August 2018.

"Bone Deep." Pen of the Damned, July 2018.

"Say (Part II)." Previously unpublished.

ACKNOWLEDGMENTS

I HAVE A LOT of people to thank for this book.

To my parents, Ruth C. Algee and the late Griffin B. Algee, who provided love and encouragement and imparted their own love of reading to me; and to Mrs. Wanda Richardson—librarian, mentor, and the person who introduced me to H. P. Lovecraft and helped set my on this path: to them I owe the utmost gratitude.

Thanks also, immensely, to Beth Renard, Heather Cupples, Zainah Alrujaib (you told me so), Julia Benally, Ian Sputnik, Nathan Hystad, Rob Campbell, Dan Foytik, and Nelson W. Pyles for being my sounding boards and ideamongers. Thanks to my editors along the way: Lester Smith, Barry Skelhorn, Lee A. Forman, Gloria Bobrowicz, none of this would have been possible without you.

Last but not least, my thanks to Don Noble for the amazing cover work, and to William Holloway, Sarah Read, and Gwendolyn Kiste for the camaraderie and kind words.

Scarlett R. Algee
March 2020

ABOUT THE AUTHOR

SCARLETT R. ALGEE'S fiction has been published by *Body Parts Magazine*, *Bards and Sages Quarterly*, Pen of the Damned, and The Wicked Library, among other places. Her short story "Dark Music," written for the podcast "The Lift," was a 2016 Parsec Awards finalist, and her flash-fiction piece "Bone Deep" is a 2020 Pushcart Prize nominee. She lives in rural Tennessee with a beagle cleverly disguised as a Hound of Tindalos, and skulks on Twitter at @scarlettralgee.